THE ROBESPIERRE SERIAL

Also by Nicholas Luard / The Warm and Golden War

Nicholas Luard

The Robespierre Serial

HARCOURT BRACE JOVANOVICH
New York and London

Copyright © 1975 by Nicholas Luard

All rights reserved. No part of this publication may be reproduced or transmitted in any form or by any means, electronic or mechanical, including photocopy, recording, or any information storage and retrieval system, without permission in writing from the publsher.

Printed in the United States of America

Library of Congress Cataloging in Publication Data

Luard, Nicholas.
The Robespierre serial.

I. Title.
PZ4.L9256Ro3 [PR6062.U12]   823'.9'14   74-22081
ISBN 0-15-178319-5

First American edition

B C D E

for Christopher Logue

THE ROBESPIERRE SERIAL

1

Madrid

Only one of the passengers on the arriving London flight was a woman—and she was the wrong woman.

Carswell knew that as soon as he saw her on top of the ramp.

Suede coat, dark glasses, hair lifting in the wind. She stood there, hand touching the scarf at her throat, aware of the men turning to glance back as they crossed the tarmac to the bus. Then she started down the steps. Young, almost certainly attractive (he couldn't tell for sure because of the distance between the observation terrace and the runway), momentarily important—the focus of attention as the others waited for her to join them inside.

Carswell turned away.

No one, least of all a group of men, would stand waiting expectantly for the other woman, the right one. Maybe a bunch of typing pool secretaries once, not even them now. Carswell had never seen her but he knew exactly what she'd be like. Something over fifty, thickening, grey hair coiled neatly in a bun above a thoroughly sensible and very dowdy travelling coat, probably weighed down by a bulging string-bag in either hand. Hurrying, perhaps, weary and a little nervous—as if it was the first time she'd flown.

But above all anonymous. Anonymous. That of course was what made her the perfect courier.

'Any luck?'

Ramón, who'd driven him out to Barajas in the section van, had come out of the café at the back of the terrace.

'No.'

'Hell—!'

He stopped beside Carswell, blowing on a glass of coffee cupped in his hands.

'Well, there are two more scheduled flights. I'll check the board to see if they've got any charters or excursions coming in.'

Carswell shook his head. 'No point. The excursions get sold out months in advance. And they wouldn't put her on a charter; it means registering forty-eight hours before and all manner of complications. It'll be one of the scheduled runs.'

'Christ, you'd think at least they could get themselves organized enough to give us the flight number.'

Carswell shrugged. 'I didn't see the Telex, but from what the resident said it sounded as if they were cobbling something together at the last moment. They've probably had her booked on every flight all day and she's still sitting in the waiting-room while they type up the expenses instructions.'

Ramón finished his coffee and snorted contemptuously. 'I'll tell you something. If I got the peanut-stall franchise in Las Ventas, I wouldn't trust that lot to manage it without panicking.'

He put the glass down on the parapet wall and glanced at his watch.

'You want another of these? We've got twenty minutes before the next one lands—that's if the third world war doesn't break out first.'

Carswell nodded. Then, as Ramón went back to the café, he swung round towards the airfield again.

The bus must have been held up at the perimeter road, because it was just pulling in below him by the arrival gates. One of the men helped the girl down the steps; she smiled quickly, then she walked, ahead of them all this time into the hall. She was carrying an expensive hand-stitched leather bag and she had long well-shaped legs.

Carswell lifted his head and grinned, his reflection hovering across the glass shield on the parapet; wispy sun-paled hair, grey eyes webbed with wrinkles, tanned face framed by the flapping collar of his raincoat.

A TWA Boeing was coming in to land, wheels smoking as it touched the ground. The hills beyond were flanked with snow and the rising wind mingled with the roar of the engines.

He fastened his top button and gazed across the runways.

While Carswell didn't share Ramón's total cynicism about London, in a way the Spaniard was right. London did have a tendency to panic. It happened about once a year, just as it had done yesterday: a priority Telex through the embassy to the resident, a message that a courier-delivered brief had to be collected from the airport (the Service used pensioned secretaries just as the Foreign Office employed portly retired colonels for its "Queen's Messengers"), then the farcical anticlimax of carrying out the instructions—a week's surveillance of a philandering French diplomat or a night-action assessment of the Spanish army's capacity to invade Gibraltar.

'Here—'

Carswell was still smiling when Ramón came back with two steaming glasses.

'What do you want to do if she's not on this one?' Ramón was rummaging in his pocket for a pack of Camels. 'Back to Calle Ruiz—or sit out the three hours until the last flight gets in?'

Carswell took one of the crumpled cigarettes and leant over Ramón's lighter.

The section house was in Calle Ruiz, a small lopsided building smelling of fruit, halfway up the narrow street near the city centre. It was a very small section: apart from the resident, who worked in another office, there was only himself, Ramón, a secretary and Pepe Vasquez, the gravel-voiced Basque who handled political intelligence.

Normally either he or Ramón was the last to leave. If the courier missed the next flight and they drove back through the rush-hour traffic before coming out again to meet the final one, they'd be on the road for most of the three hours. Tonight one of the other two could lock up for a change.

'We'll stay here.' Carswell tapped the tip of his cigarette on the ledge. 'Can we find a set down there?'

He gestured at the main concourse below them.

'Sure.' Ramón nodded. 'They'll have one in the international lounge. Anyway, I know an Iberia chief steward who keeps one in his locker.'

'Okay.' Carswell propped himself against the parapet. 'Give it ten minutes, and if she's not on it, that's what we'll do.'

He and Ramón had played chess almost every evening since he'd joined the section twelve years earlier. Afterwards, he'd go back to his three-room apartment, cook himself a meal, then go out again—getting up at dawn, as he invariably did, Carswell liked to be in bed by midnight. He might go to the bodega across the road where a new flamenco guitarist had started that week, or he could try for another game in one of the cafés further down the street.

That was one of the advantages of a Madrid posting. The other sections might have the drama and the urgency. Madrid was a backwater. Madrid was chess and the voice of a *cante jondo* singer at night and glasses of yellow manzanilla on a raw-wood table and long days of walking, when the section house closed down, in the high sierras to the south.

A slow, solitary private life. The life Carswell had settled for years ago.

'So what's it going to be this time?'

Ramón had rested his arms on the wall; his cigarette was

slanted down between his teeth and the dregs of the coffee were clouding in the glass at his elbow.

'If it's not nuclear Armageddon at dusk?' Carswell grinned. 'Maybe London's out of paper clips.'

'Jesus!' Ramón shook his head. 'Listen, if I got the Las Ventas peanut franchise—hey, I said that, didn't I?'

'Yes.'

'Well, I still wouldn't. Those London briefs, I got a nine-year-old nephew who could do them in his head cycling back from school!'

'Maybe this time it'll be different.'

'You mean, maybe this time God didn't make those little green apples!'

As Ramón swore, Carswell, still smiling, turned to watch the lowering sun touch the distant snow-drifts with rose.

A few minutes later the next to last flight of the day touched down from London. The courier was the fifth passenger to appear on the ramp. Unmistakeable—precisely as Carswell had guessed she'd be.

He went down to the arrivals hall, watched her deposit a package in a self-operated left-luggage box, then called a porter, gave him a card and a hundred-peseta note and sent him over to where she was standing by the taxi-rank. The porter returned with a key. Carswell opened the box, removed the package and clambered into the section van alongside Ramón.

Across the top of the package, in small lower-case lettering, were stencilled the words "Robespierre Serial: Manifest and Transit Documents." Below them someone had written in the name of the resident.

The Robespierre serial, as Carswell discovered when he went over it with the resident next morning, wasn't just one of London's annual last-minute panics. In fact, there'd been no panic at all—not until an evening in Geneva three weeks earlier.

2

Geneva

There'd been something fastidious and wary in the man's eyes which would never have risked the darkness, Handley-Reid was certain of that.

It meant that if he came, it would be within the next few minutes, before dusk fell. Handley-Reid was equally certain if the man didn't come then, he wouldn't come at all.

He walked over to the window and stood above Spencer. Outside the air was thick with rain and the light was already fading fast. Across the road a line of naked bulbs glowed above the patisserie at the corner of the Rue Vaumar.

'Where's the transfer car?'

The black Citroën, parked all day on the other side of the square, had disappeared and he couldn't see the bald-headed figure of the embassy driver.

'He's just had to move it, sir. It's the residents coming back from work; they've got permits for the parking-places.'

Spencer put down the binoculars to rub his face. The rubber eye-pieces had pressed white circles in the skin on his nose and his head was aching.

'He's coming round again now, sir.'

The Citroën appeared at the end of the square. It drove slowly past below them, turned left before the Rue Vaumar and vanished again behind the trees. Handley-Reid glimpsed it through the leaves; the driver had found a space ten yards down from the café and was backing the car between two vans.

The café door swung shut, and Handley-Reid turned to look towards the Cercle. Apart from the Citroën there were four other cars stationed round the square.

Two were in the narrow parallel streets which ran down towards the lake highway at the southern end; depending on the final choice of route to the airport, one of them would act as the convoy leader. The Citroën would follow, with Darley, the head of the Riyadh section, beside the passenger on the rear seat; the man had insisted that Darley be with him constantly from the moment of the transfer until the flight reached London. Handley-Reid and Spencer would come next in the rented Peugeot, which they'd left outside the pharmacy downstairs.

Finally, there was Clouvain, the Swiss resident. He'd been waiting at the Cercle since midday. From there he could see right up the Avenue Béarne almost to the Loti itself. The man had been typically elusive about the time he planned to leave the hotel: "All the arrangements have their own complexities," he'd said, "not merely ours; it is impossible for me to be precise." He'd even insisted on using his own Cadillac for the journey between the hotel and the square.

Clouvain's task was to pick up the Cadillac as it reached the Cercle and escort it down the Rue Vaumar to the café where the transfer would be made. Darley was waiting for him there.

Handley-Reid moved away from the table and crossed the room. It was a dark musty apartment with badly fitting doors and a creaking floor. The rain had intensified the smell of damp and there was condensation on the silver-gilt mounts of the photographs round the walls: plump Geneva matrons with wire-tight mouths, sullen-faced burghers, stiff little children in crinolines, all with runnels of water trickling down their yellowed faces.

He half turned to face the empty fireplace, lit a cigarette and smoked it slowly down to the stub. Then he glanced at the window again. Spencer's shoulders were a blur against the glass and the rain was shining with a grainy translucence in the light of the street lamps.

'Everyone still there, Spencer?'

Handley-Reid pushed himself away from the wall.

'Yes, sir.' Spencer's voice was muffled under the binoculars. 'Mr. Darley went over to the transfer car a few minutes ago, but he's back in the café now. Monsieur Clouvain's still waiting by the awning—'

'That's fine,' Handley-Reid cut him off. 'Because what you're going to do now is get out there and tell them it's all over.'

Spencer swung round, his face a startled white oval in the darkness.

'It's over, Spencer, finished, ended.' The words came out flat and hard. 'He's not coming. No, I haven't the slightest idea what's happened; maybe the little bastard just changed his mind. But he's not coming, understand? So go and tell the whole bloody lot of them. I want Mr. Darley to follow us. The others can go back to the embassy.'

'Now, sir?'

'Yes, Spencer, right this bloody moment.'

As Spencer scrambled to his feet and hurried out, Handley-Reid swung himself up onto the table and lit another cigarette.

Eight months. Eight months of the most careful and elaborate planning he'd ever given to a single operation. Eight months which had ended a few minutes earlier in the darkness of a rain-filled April evening in nothing, nothing at all. He didn't even know yet what had happened. For the moment it didn't matter. He would find out.

3

Geneva

'I want to know, Mr. Darley.'

It was fifteen minutes after they'd left the apartment. Darley had followed them from the square and Clouvain had joined the procession at the Cercle, tucking himself in behind the Citroën so that the three cars nosed slowly in line through the streaming darkness, with the shop lights glittering on either side of the avenue.

Then they'd stopped at the Loti. Handley-Reid had wound down his window as Darley appeared at the side of the car. Darley stood there for a moment, thin and sandy-haired, with steel-rimmed glasses and a vague freckled face. He tugged at the knot of his tie and nodded.

'I'm not sure how long it'll take.'

'As long as you bloody well need.'

'I suppose it's conceivable he'll refuse to see me.'

'If he does, send in a message saying you'll stay outside all night, all week if necessary. And if that doesn't work you can tell him I'll personally walk straight through the door and tear his windpipe out.'

'Yes, of course.'

Darley's face vanished. A few moments later Spencer saw him in the driving-mirror. He spoke to one of the commissionaires, shouldered his way through the crowd on the steps and disappeared into the hotel.

Spencer glanced uneasily across the car. Handley-Reid was sitting opposite him in the passenger seat, a tall, hard-framed man with the high colour of some hunting landowner from the shires; dark hair edged with grey, a spare bony face, cornflower-blue eyes whose whites were veined with scarlet. He was wearing a tight-cut Donegal tweed suit with a cream shirt, and the red and blue bars on his Brigade of Guards tie were so muted that from a few yards they looked a solid black.

Sprawled back against the window with one brilliantly polished shoe propped against the dashboard, he might have been a caricature of an English gentleman. Yet Handley-Reid was very different from the studiedly elegant image he invariably presented.

Handley-Reid had a first-class-honours degree in Oriental studies from Oxford, a legendary war record as a long-range desert patrol commander and a knowledge of the Arab world unrivalled in British intelligence circles. They were attributes which, as controller of the Secret Intelligence Service's Middle Eastern sections for the past ten years, had allowed him to operate as if he were running a private feudal kingdom. He also had, as Spencer quickly discovered in two years as his assistant, a bitter brooding cast of mind, an acid contempt for the bureaucratic timidity of modern intelligence-gathering procedures, and a limitless capacity for resentment.

Brilliant, arrogant, vindictive, hard-drinking and hair-trigger-tempered, Handley-Reid was always an unpredictable and demanding superior. Tense with anger as he was now, his very presence on the other side of the car made Spencer shift uncomfortably in his seat.

He'd said in the apartment that the serial was over. It wasn't; Spencer knew that. The man's failure to keep the rendezvous had touched the rawest nerves of Handley-Reid's vanity. The Robespierre serial wouldn't be over until someone had paid in blood for what had happened.

Spencer shook his head and concentrated on the driving-mirror. People were still pressed together under the canopy, and the courtyard was jammed with taxis. Then he saw Darley again—running this time as he came down the steps and headed for the car.

Darley was panting when he stopped and his tie had slipped back under his collar.

'He's not there.'

For an instant Handley-Reid thought he must have been wrong about the darkness after all; that the man had left later than he'd believed and might already be waiting at the Cercle.

'We'd better get straight back then—'

'No, he's checked out, Colonel,' Darley interrupted him. 'He went just after midday. All of them went, the women and everyone. He paid his bill, told the hotel to call some taxis and they just left.'

There was a brief silence. A pool of rainwater spilled off the shoulder of Darley's jacket and ran down his shirt, making a dark stain on the light, slightly dirty cloth. He glanced down, mildly surprised, and tried to brush it away with his hand.

Then Handley-Reid said, 'Did you find out where?'

Darley shook his head. 'The only people who might know are the day commissionaires. I'm afraid they've gone off duty. But it's somewhere inside the city; they've got a special firm they use for journeys to the airport, and it wasn't the one they called. The desk clerk remembers that.'

'Right.' Handley-Reid looked at Spencer. 'We'll go straight back to the Vendôme—'

He looked at Darley again.

'I want you there, Mr. Darley, and tell Monsieur Clouvain to join us too. I don't care how long it takes, but we're going to find him.'

They pulled away abruptly, leaving Darley standing under the trees with the rain still pattering onto his shoulders.

* * *

It was almost two the next morning before Handley-Reid was sure he knew what had happened.

They'd gathered in his suite at the Vendôme as soon as they got back from the Loti, without even pausing to change their rain-soaked clothes. Spencer was reminded of a party of duck hunters after a day on the marshes. He'd taken off his jacket and hung it over the back of a chair, where it steamed gently in the room's warmth; Darley, steam rising from his jacket too, was leaning against the bedside table smoking a crumpled cigarette; Clouvain was sitting on the bed drinking from a pigskin flask of whiskey; while Handley-Reid was searching through a lightweight metal filing box that might have been a gun-case.

For a moment in the silence there was a pervading sense of physical tiredness, of mud flats and a dawn tide, duck flighting high against an east wind, spent cartridges glinting on the frozen crust of a reed bed.

Then Handley-Reid stood up, and instantly everything changed.

'Right, gentlemen—'

There were two white patches high on his cheeks.

He questioned Darley first. Then, when Darley had failed to provide any plausible explanation for what the man might have done, he turned to Clouvain.

'Well, Colonel,' Clouvain said. 'For this moment we work on the assumption he is still here in Genève—'

A big plump grey-faced man with cropped ginger hair, Clouvain was an outsider in the company of the other three; as Swiss resident, he was responsible solely to the European controller, and he'd been brought into the serial only a few weeks earlier, when Geneva had been chosen for the transfer.

Now he pushed himself forward until he was sitting on the edge of the bed.

'So we start with the Loti. Fortunate, maybe, that I know their commissionaires. We use the hotel much for business and

I think they will help us. That Arab, the women, the taxis; they could not have missed him leaving—'

Clouvain shook his watch down his wrist and shrugged.

'Time, Colonel Handley-Reid, time. This is our problem. I have to visit them, locate their addresses first, after ask questions what they do remember. Then we have the airports and the land frontiers—thirty-nine highway posts on four borders. However I see what we can do.'

Clouvain, who'd left the hotel after the meeting ended, telephoned first at ten. The airport check had proved negative, but he'd obtained the addresses of both the Loti's day commissionaires and was leaving immediately to interview them.

At eleven-thirty he called again. This time he was speaking from the manager's office in a hotel called the Pierre Arvois. He'd gone there straight from the home of the second Loti commissionaire, who'd helped the party into their taxis and heard the man give the Arvois as their destination.

Three suites had been booked there a week earlier. The party had arrived soon after midday, spent an hour in the hotel, then they'd left again in a convoy of rented cars. The cars had been hired with chauffeurs for the day and the man had refused to say where they were going next.

'I'm making guesses, of course, Colonel,' Clouvain added, 'but I believe they are making in the direction for the border, not merely changing hotels again. Otherwise, I think they would use taxis. Also, if it is the border, then I expect they will be met there; this could explain why the cars are hired only for the day. Anyway, I try to check.'

Handley-Reid put down the telephone, glanced round at Darley and Spencer, and curtly told them to go to bed.

Clouvain's third call came through at ten to two.

Late in the afternoon five Hertz Mercedes had arrived at the police control post on the Swiss-French frontier south of Geneva near Annemasse. The party, three men and five women with a considerable quantity of baggage, had been travelling on Saudi Arabian diplomatic passports. The passports were all in order and the eight people had passed through within fifteen minutes.

Fifty yards away on the French side of the border the party had transferred to another group of cars; the Swiss police inspector, who'd been watching them out of curiosity, thought the new cars were also Mercedes but wasn't sure because of the mist on the pass. Ten minutes later the convoy disappeared down the Grenoble road and the Hertz cars re-entered Switzerland.

'There's something else which maybe interests you, Colonel,' Clouvain said. 'We have here in Genève a man, what we call a *dixeur,* that is a man of many things, with the name Beiren. He crosses often into France and many times he brings me back cognac. He is not a friend but I know him and maybe one day he hopes of things from me. Anyway—'

Clouvain laughed. 'After we have discussed the cars, the inspecteur says I must be up so late because I am drinking cognac; he too knows Beiren and it is a sort of a joke between us. And it seems that Beiren also crosses the border today. He spends some time in France, comes back, waits at the post until the party has gone through, then he leaves for Genève again.'

'And what's the significance of that?'

'Well, Beiren is very close with the Americans. I cannot know for sure but good sources say he is the local communications operative for the CIA. I think maybe he is there in case of any difficulties at the post.'

'Thank you, Monsieur Clouvain. I'm most grateful for everything you've done.'

'Maybe there is something else tonight?'

'No. You've answered the last question.'

Handley-Reid rang off, sat for a moment gazing at the drawn curtains, then went into the corridor and walked down to Spencer's room.

'Wake up!'

He shook him roughly by the shoulder. Spencer sat upright in the darkness.

'Yes, sir.' His voice was furred with sleep.

'Book us on the first flight to Paris in the morning. Then get hold of the embassy duty officer and send these out on their Telex. There'll be an answer to the first one, which he can telephone through as soon as it comes in—'

Spencer turned on the light, fumbled for his notebook and took down the messages. Then, yawning and swearing, he began to dress.

Handley-Reid didn't go to bed when he returned to his own room. He removed his jacket, turned off all the lights, lay down on the bed with a pack of cigarettes beside him, and stayed there chain-smoking until dawn.

4

London

'A manufactured threat to his life which we allow them to discover for themselves. And then when they guess an operation's been mounted, to realize the situation requires our help in aborting—'

Handley-Reid nodded. 'What I'd classify as covert provocative action, Director.'

'Covert provocative action—'

The Director repeated the phrase slowly, resting the tips of his fingers against each other.

He was a small, sleek, fastidious man, a career diplomat who'd headed the Service for less than a year and who was still patently overawed by the cadre of former professional soldiers like Handley-Reid who constituted its senior staff.

'Well,' he continued, 'everything's going to depend on finding the right man. Without him the whole idea's academic. And it won't be easy; I don't need tell you that, Colonel. In fact, I think it could well founder there—'

Handley-Reid listened in silence while he rambled on. Without the right man, the Robespierre serial was obviously over. But if he could be found, the Director had already implicitly committed himself to sanctioning its new coda.

Handley-Reid had no doubt at all that he'd find him.

The idea had finally come to Handley-Reid on the flight back from Paris to London earlier that evening.

The day had started in Geneva when the embassy telephoned through the answer to the first of the previous night's Telexes while he and Spencer were having breakfast: Vavasseur, the European head of the CIA, would meet him at midday in a hotel on the Left Bank off the Boulevard St.-Germain. There was an Air France Caravelle which left at ten and arrived at Orly an hour later. It gave them exactly the right amount of time.

As soon as they took off, Handley-Reid rang for the stewardess and ordered a large vodka. He always drank in the morning; it seemed to have no effect on him except to heighten the colour of his face. With the ice clinking in the glass and Spencer asleep across the aisle, his mouth half open and his tallow hair falling forward over his eyes, he systematically reviewed the serial from the arrival of Darley's guarded letter.

Delivered safe-hand by courier eight months before, the letter stated briefly that Darley had been approached by an individual who'd indicated he might be interested in political asylum. There was no name, just the comment that "he's potentially the most valuable source of political and economic intelligence we've ever had the opportunity of acquiring."

As the capital of Saudi Arabia, Riyadh was the most important oil city in the world. A refugee from the country's ruling circles, and it was at least implicit that the man was a member of them, would be a priceless intelligence prize—even if he only half measured up to Darley's description.

It was two months before Handley-Reid learned the man's identity. Then he realized that, if anything, Darley had understated his value.

Sheikh Salah Fouad Ibn Saud Samir. Nephew by marriage of the deposed king. Educated at Le Rosey and the Harvard Business School. Former minister for development of internal resources, twice Saudi Arabian delegate to Pan-Arab conferences, five times principal negotiator on drilling-concession renewals. A millionaire, a compulsive womanizer, a fanatical follower of the ancient desert sports of antelope hunting, camel racing and falconry.

The profile might have fit any oil-rich Arab of Samir's generation. Yet Samir was different. As different from the stereotype of his biography as was Handley-Reid from the die-stamped image of an English gentleman.

Samir was also a Marxist. He'd appeared as a peace counsellor to the republican side in the Yemeni civil war; he was a friend of Qaddafi; Yasir Arafat trusted him alone among the Arab monarchists. But for twenty years he'd also managed to preserve the confidence of his own family, the Saudi Arabian monarchy. Even in the turbulent and contradictory world of Arab politics, it was an extraordinary achievement.

It meant that he had access to the inner councils of both sides of modern Arabia, to a spectrum of people, policies and movements which spanned the entire range of Arab affairs from the high command of Black September to the court of King Faisal.

And now he wanted political asylum. His reasons were straightforward enough. Over the past decade the mood of the Arab world had changed dramatically: conflicts had become more bitter, power struggles more complex and ruthless, tensions between rich and poor, right and left, feudal and modern, increasingly violent and explosive.

The effects on Samir, even if the Marxist dimension hadn't made his position unique, were predictable. He'd summarized them for Darley at their first meeting.

'There's an Arab proverb, Mr. Darley—knowledge is an excellent tonic for the mind but a deadly poison to the body. I, Mr. Darley, have a great deal of knowledge, for my body's health far, far too much. That's what interests you whom I count as my friends. Regrettably, it is also what interests a large number of other people to whom my continued well-being has become a considerable embarrassment.'

It had taken six months of complex secret negotiations before Samir seemed satisfied that his well-being would be better guaranteed in Britain than anywhere else.

Finally, less than three weeks ago, a second safe-hand letter had arrived from Darley: agreement had been reached on all major conditions; Samir would travel to Geneva ostensibly to attend the Wetzlein clinic; providing the remaining details were worked out to his satisfaction, the transfer would be made two weeks later.

By then time had become a key factor on both sides. For Samir, the growing challenge to his role in Arab affairs had hardened into specific threats against his life. To Handley-Reid, it was the long-heralded Pan-Arab conference which created the urgency. Most of the major decisions would bear little relation to the fiery propaganda communiqués handed down from the platform when the conference convened in May.

The real alliances and agreements, the policies hewn out in secret debate since the Yom Kippur war, would remain unrevealed until much later, when they'd gradually emerge to alter the whole political landscape of the Middle East—and at the same time the dimensions of the world energy crisis.

'Six months' clear use of that information—and we'll have a head start on tackling the oil shortage that'll take the rest of Europe years to catch up. To the Americans, of course, it would literally be priceless.'

The assessment was the Under-Secretary of State's when the existence of the Robespierre serial was first communicated to the Foreign Office.

Now that information and everything else that Samir knew, for the critical period of time before it became public knowledge, would belong exclusively to the Americans.

Unless, of course, Handley-Reid could devise some way of keeping the serial open. By the time they landed in Paris his anger towards Samir had evaporated.

In its place he felt a cold objective hatred.

It was raining at Orly as it had been in Geneva.

A member of the Paris station, a young cypher clerk, drove them into the centre of the city. He'd brought with him a file, updated until ten that morning, containing the results of the section's search for the cars—the subject of Handley-Reid's first Telex from the hotel.

Handley-Reid had just finished reading through it when they reached the address off the Boulevard St.-Germain. Vavasseur was waiting for him in the bar. Apart from the barman he was the only person in the room.

'Charles, how pleasant!'

He ordered a drink and Handley-Reid sat down opposite him by the stone fireplace.

Vavasseur. Handley-Reid had first met him as a young counterintelligence officer with Eisenhower's headquarters group at the end of the war. Now, thirty years later—the last eight of them as Allen Dulles's own appointee to over-all controller of the CIA's European operations—he was plump, bland, black-suited, with a heavy gold watch-chain glittering against his waistcoat.

Leaning back in his chair, hands folded over his stomach, eyes smiling behind half-moon glasses, he might have been a successful merchant, a prosperous grocer or haberdasher from the suburbs who'd lived in Paris all his life and whom the city fitted like a glove. Even his pronounciation of Handley-Reid's first name had the guttural inflexion of Marly or St.-Cloud.

Handley-Reid found the affectation as distasteful as the benignly patronizing attitude Vavasseur had adopted towards him ever since they'd first known each other.

'But nostalgia didn't bring you here, Charles. It was—what did you call him? Robespierre, no?'

They'd been talking casually for ten minutes when Vavasseur put down his glass and leant forward.

Handley-Reid sipped his vodka and said nothing.

'Oh, don't be offended; of course he's told us that. No—' he held up a small round hand as Handley-Reid opened his mouth—'let me tell you. You're angry and aggrieved, Charles; let's not mince words. And, my God, you have good reason. So much work, so much time, so much money. And then at the last moment he changes his mind, he comes to us instead. I'll tell you one thing: we made no approach to him; it was his own decision. You won't believe it, but it was so.'

'I don't believe it.'

'No.' Vavasseur shook his head regretfully. 'Still, it's happened. And now no doubt you'd like access to him. The "common interest," no? It was so easy once, Charles, wasn't it? Well, let's hope something of it still remains. While I myself don't have the disposing of the gentleman, I'll pass on your request immediately to those who do—'

'You'll pass it on,' Handley-Reid interrupted him, 'and your bloody State Department will prevaricate, temporize, lie. So by the time we're finally allowed to talk to him, what he knows will be worth slightly less than a handful of bazaar rumours—'

Handley-Reid broke off. Then he asked abruptly, 'Has it occurred to you that we could find him?'

'Find him—?'

For a moment Vavasseur looked startled.

'At eight-fifteen last night he crossed into France. His party transferred from the Swiss-rented Mercedes into a convoy of cars you probably sent up from Fontainebleau—'

Handley-Reid recited the details of the Paris station's report.

He didn't know why he was doing it, any more than he knew why he'd asked the question which had startled Vavasseur. But he held stubbornly to the conviction that something would emerge from the conversation which would provide the key he was looking for.

'Their final destination?' Handley-Reid shrugged. 'Obviously we don't know yet. The Riviera, perhaps. Alternatively, they could swing north up the Rhone valley and head for the Loire, where you have all those expensive "language laboratory" houses—isn't that what you call them now? It doesn't matter. We're—observing. We'll find out.'

There was a short silence. Vavasseur reached out his hand and rubbed it along the gleaming brass fender of the grate.

'I can save you the trouble, Charles. Not France—Spain. They'll cross the border near Perpignan this evening. Then they'll vanish. You're obviously aware of his phobia about flying. Well, for the final stage we've convinced him it's necessary —not even your admirable Paris station's going to follow him in the air. I wish, frankly, we were flying him much further, but we're not. We're taking him to the place he's chosen and when he gets there we'll take the necessary steps to protect him—'

Vavasseur looked up frowning.

'Yes, I suppose it's conceivable you could eventually find him, Charles. It'll take time, I promise you, much longer than the few weeks before this Cairo conference opens. Yet we're too old to play hide and seek, you and I—'

'We may be, others aren't,' Handley-Reid said. 'And whoever it is, I doubt it'll take anything like as long as you believe.'

Handley-Reid's interruption had been spontaneous, unconsidered. Yet as soon as he'd finished speaking, he knew instantly that he'd found what he was after. Vavasseur knew it too. For a few moments they both sat in silence.

It was possible that even now, barely twenty-four hours after Samir had checked out of the Loti, the news had reached Riyadh and his enemies were already planning to silence him. If they could discover his sanctuary—and from what Vavasseur had said the place was his own choice, made perhaps months earlier—then it was inevitable an attempt on his life would be mounted before the conference began.

'Charles, you're an unfailing source of pleasure.' Vavasseur chuckled happily. 'I grow old and fat and sleepy. Then out of the blue you return—as Machiavellian as ever—and everything comes back, all those marvellous times we had. I even start to believe in myself again. Of course I understand—'

He lifted his hand and called for the barman.

'And I've not the slightest doubt that if news of someone looking for our little friend reaches you before me, then sheer altruism will prompt you to pass it on, rather than any remote thought of encouraging me to let you see him before the conference starts!'

The Paris-London shuttle was stacked above Heathrow before Handley-Reid decided how the mutually acknowledged realization, which had come out of his meeting with Vavasseur, could be used to keep the Robespierre serial open.

The trigger was the sheer rugged mass of Spain on the airline's route map; the dark-brown contours of the northern mountains, the great fissured sweep of the Castillian plateau in the centre, the bright green valleys and plains, serrated with other mountain ranges, which ran down to the south. Wherever Samir had elected to hide, it would be in open country. Handley-Reid knew he could count on that. To an Arab of his class and background, prolonged city life would be unendurable— even more so now as an exile than before.

Yet to a dedicated professional killer—and there'd be plenty of those available to his enemies—that same countryside could not have been bettered as a hunting-ground. For Vavasseur the problems in guaranteeing Samir's safety were enormous. The very possibility of a gunman at loose in those hills and valleys was a security nightmare in itself. Knowing the possibility had become fact was something far different.

If that happened, there'd be every incentive to ask for the Service's co-operation in seeing the threat was neutralized. And if the price was to share the intelligence Samir had brought with him, then Samir alive was infinitely preferable under any conditions to Samir dead.

The problem, as the Director pointed out when Handley-Reid put the idea to him that evening, was to find the right man. The search took most of the following day.

Spencer eventually turned up the file in the S-list archives late in the afternoon. The archives held the Service's records of every individual who'd been linked with some form of terrorism or subversion. Many contained no more than a single sheet of paper with a name at the top, a couple of references and the relevant dates. Others had as much as a dozen pages of information.

The S file on a forty-eight-year-old Belgian called Jean LeKahn consisted of three entries.

The first had been made as a result of a special investigation by the Service itself a few months after the death of Patrice Lumumba in 1967. The Ministry of Defence had asked for a list of the Belgian officers responsible for Lumumba's murder. Ten weeks later the head of the Kinshasa station had come up with seven names. LeKahn's was last on the list. Against it were the words: "Belgian national with Lebanese mother."

The next paragraph was datelined Limassol, November 1970. The source was a Cyprus newspaper report of the murder of a German businessman, who'd been shot down as he was leaving his apartment in the Avenida Kyrenia. The cutting stated that the police were anxious to interview a "Mr. J. LeKahn, a realestate developer, with whom the murdered man was due to have lunch that day."

Underneath, one of the clerks in the intelligence analysis bureau had written that the German was believed to be an agent of the Shabak arm of Shin Beth, the Israeli counter-terrorist organization.

The third was simply a computer print-out giving LeKahn's name and two Marseilles addresses. The same hand as the one above had added a note that LeKahn's was one of eleven names which fitted the profile of the arms supplier for a planned Black September raid.

'It's a bit scrappy, isn't it?' The Director stared at the sheet of paper. 'I mean, God knows what he could actually turn out to be like.'

'He seems to fulfill the main conditions, Director,' Handley-Reid said patiently. 'A Lebanese mother; links with at least two other murders; strong indications of a connection with Arab terrorism; and above all nothing whatsoever to connect him with us. There won't, of course, be any direct approach until everything's been checked out. I've got Colonel Cazenove from Treasury liaison in mind for that.'

'Colonel Cazenove?'

'He's very experienced in free-lance-agent evaluation. He did Holland during the war and the Greek trouble after that.' Handley-Reid paused. 'All very much before your time, I'm afraid, Director.'

The Director sat forward over his desk, frowning and plucking unhappily at the scarlet tab on LeKahn's file.

'If that's so—and frankly I don't regard even an implied commitment yet—then how would you see the rest of the operation being structured?'

'Completely at arm's length and using what we used to call a "ghost section"—'

Handley-Reid's voice became brisker. He'd spent considerable time over the mechanics of the operation and he explained them well, larding the description with the obscure jargon phrases which the Director found so impressive.

The ghost section would have three arms: himself as co-ordinator; Cazenove to recruit, brief and run the man; and Mather, who headed the military capabilities bureau, to handle the signals. Then there'd be Spencer, who'd act as a field communications post, and finally an escort to monitor LeKahn's progress. The choice of the last was a detail which could be left to the end.

Both Cazenove and Mather were old-guard Service hands like himself. As he talked, Handley-Reid suddenly realized how much like a wartime mission it would be. The same faces, the same urgency, the same rapid decisions, the same sense of improvisation as one put together the elements for some lightning raid that had so often achieved more in a single hour than the ponderous minutely planned advance of an armoured brigade in a week.

By the time he finished, even the Director had caught some of his enthusiasm.

'I must confess I rather like it, Colonel. Of course, not the sort of thing one would countenance in any but the most extreme circumstances. But as a way of tackling the *de facto* situation, it's certainly got, well—'

He leant back in his chair snapping his fingers.

'Flair, I suppose. Even if, as I said yesterday, you fellows do frequently scare the daylights out of a chairbound old codger like myself!'

He laughed. For once Handley-Reid smiled back.

Cazenove flew out to Marseilles the next day.

He was away forty-eight hours. Thirty minutes after he returned, the operation was formally sanctioned; LeKahn had accepted the contract for the mission and the Director had given his consent to its being mounted immediately.

'How do you rate him, Peter?'

'Christ knows what he did to Lumumba, but in a way I rather took to him,' Cazenove said. 'Thick-set fellow, bald as a coot, says very little, watches you all the time. I wouldn't fancy him much as a son-in-law, but for what you need I doubt he could be better.'

'Did he haggle much?'

'Not really. I had to go to the limit, but he's a professional, knows his price. He wasn't going to settle for less.'

Handley-Reid nodded. 'And how did he feel about it all?'

'Difficult to say.' Cazenove shrugged. 'He understood it, all right. God knows, it's hardly going to overtax him. I mean, what's he basically got to do? Look purposeful and keep moving, that's about all. The only important thing is that he's out there to back up the signals. Vavasseur can't afford to shilly-shally around, just too bloody risky—'

Cazenove broke off and paused. A dark aquiline man with thinning hair, his grey suit was almost identical to Handley-Reid's and his shoes had the same mahogany burnish.

Then he laughed. 'I'll tell you something, Charles. He already knew quite a bit about Samir. Well, one could have guessed that. I don't think it's beyond the bounds of possibility that LeKahn will actually discover where he's hidden.'

'Christ Almighty! Well, just so long as he doesn't forget what he's meant to be doing and start taking pot-shots at him—'

'Don't worry! LeKahn's been used to knocking over people for free. To be actually paid *not* to kill someone, that could be the start of a whole new and damn sight more attractive career. He won't get it back to front!'

Handley-Reid laughed too. Then he said, 'Any problems about the schedule?'

Cazenove shook his head. 'Suits him fine. He needs a few days to sort out what he calls his yacht-broking business. Then on Monday he flies to Beirut, two days there, Riyadh on Wednesday evening, back to Marseilles via Athens on Sunday, and he sets off the following Tuesday. This is the first part of his route—'

Handley-Reid leant forward as Cazenove picked up a map from the floor, and began running his finger along Route National 7 west of Marseilles.

By Friday evening they were ready.

LeKahn's Middle Eastern trip, which prefaced the actual mission, started immediately after the weekend when he flew to Beirut. The two days there and the following three in Riyadh would be crucial to the whole operation's success. Mather, whose office was in the Marylebone annexe, came over to join them in Baker Street while the details were being worked out.

It wasn't only a matter of whom LeKahn saw and when during those five days, but how intelligence about his meetings could plausibly become available—and so, reinforce rather than call into question the credibility of the signals when, as would inevitably happen, Vavasseur checked them for source.

When Mather had finished and the complex interwoven pattern of names, addresses, times and movements had been transmitted to Darley, who'd arrange the actual contacts, LeKahn's cover was as perfect as it was possible to make it. By the end of the following week anyone who retraced the Belgian's itinerary, learned whom he'd seen, what places he'd visited and at what hours, would have little doubt about the purpose of his journey.

And that would even be before they discovered he'd then left Marseilles on a route that took him due west to the Spanish border.

With Mather's contribution completed, there remained only Spencer to brief—Spencer and finally LeKahn's escort. Handley-Reid dealt with Spencer during the day. Spencer's role was essentially that of a messenger boy. He'd be based at hotels first in France and then in Spain, so that he could receive telephoned reports from LeKahn and the escort, relay them to London and in turn pass on any new instructions.

Late in the afternoon Handley-Reid went down to the second floor to see Fenton, the European controller. Large and rumpled, Fenton was yet another North Africa and Secret Operations Executive veteran—the "sand-and-sea Mafia," as they were known in the Service. He'd known about the Robespierre serial since the planned Geneva transfer and he was the only other divisional head to have been briefed on its coda.

When Handley-Reid came in, he was closing his attaché case. Fenton glanced up and grinned.

'How goes it, Charles?'

'Almost there.'

'Except you want a covert escort for your rent-a-Belgian, right?' Fenton laughed. 'I know, the Director warned me this morning. Keep an eye on him, see he stays on the straight and narrow, that sort of thing—'

Handley-Reid nodded. 'Nothing fancy, just a straightforward shadow job. No contact, out of sight, well, the old war rules. We'll give him the route, all he's got to do is see LeKahn sticks to it. Oh, and of course keep an eye out in case Vavasseur sends any of his people along when they pick up the message.'

'Well, I had a look through the files—'

Fenton went over to his desk and searched through a pile of papers.

'Try this one.' He extracted a grey folder. 'Fellow called Carswell. Did well in France for a year right at the end of the war, petered out a bit after that.'

'France? Would I remember him?'

'Doubt it.' Fenton shook his head. 'He was just a kid then. Had a spot of bother afterwards in Korea. I'd forgotten about it until I read the file again. Rather messy. He'd gone active for a while and he shot one of his own men who wouldn't move forward. The court of inquiry was inconclusive, they shoved him back to base camp as an interrogator, then we took him on again.'

'How did he come to be under you?'

'I got him when he was posted to Joint Intelligence in Brussels. Wasn't bad there, but a bit of a plodder, you know, diligent but a touch pedestrian. I shifted him to Madrid about twelve years back. Same thing there, absolutely reliable but not much go. Still—'

Fenton passed over the folder.

'He's inconspicuous, first-class linguist and knows the country like the back of his hand. Got the right combat background too. In fact, as you're playing it by the war rules, he could well be ideal as a—what the hell was it we used to call them?'

'You mean a follower?'

'Right. Just the material.' Fenton looked at his watch. 'I'm going to be late. Have a read through and let me know on Monday. If you think he'll do, I'll signal Madrid and he can be briefed out there next week.'

Handley-Reid glanced through the file as he climbed the stairs back to his office.

It added little to what Fenton had told him. John Carswell was barely seventeen when he did his year with the French resistance; it put him in his mid-forties now. Afterwards he'd switched to active soldiering and had a spell as an infantry officer. That ended with the Korean incident, and since his return to the Service he'd been with the European division, first in Brussels and subsequently in Madrid.

He'd been married briefly but the marriage had broken up at the time of the court of inquiry. Since then he'd apparently lived alone. The annual reports of his station heads confirmed Fenton's description of him as reliable and conscientious, but without initiative or ambition—"rather uninspired" was a phrase that cropped up twice. But he'd got the experience, the languages, the knowledge of the country and from the reference photograph he was certainly inconspicuous.

Handley-Reid closed the folder, tossed it into his desk drawer and turned the key. As LeKahn's covert escort, his follower, Carswell would be fine. The Madrid resident could brief him during the coming week. There was no need for Carswell to be filled in on all the ramifications of the Belgian's mission; on the strict need-to-know basis they simply didn't concern him.

From Carswell's point of view he would be merely shadowing a free-lance agent who'd been given a contract to terminate an individual the Service had declared hostile.

With the war rules to guide him, Carswell's part alone in the Robespierre serial's coda would be routine.

5

Marseilles

Carswell arrived in Marseilles on a Sunday afternoon.

It was a chill, thundery day and as he drove in from Marignane airport he could see white-capped breakers in the bay beyond the waterfront. His hotel was close to the old port in a side-street off the Canebière. By the time he checked in, the rain had moved in from the sea and was falling in dark wind-driven showers.

The instructions which had brought him there had been contained in the package he'd collected from the Barajas left-luggage box three days before. He'd gone through them with the Madrid resident, Ignacio Garcia, the following morning in a café opposite Garcia's office. The package contained an outline of the operation, details of Carswell's role as LeKahn's covert escort, procedures for communications with Spencer—who'd been coded 'Danton'—and two newly created profiles, one on LeKahn, the other on Samir.

The briefing was short, almost sketchy—Garcia himself had known nothing about the serial until the previous day's warning Telex from London. Yet if the information was sparse, the escort role was simple enough; it was one Carswell had carried out several times before, although this was the first occasion where it involved a termination mission. By the time he'd spent half an hour memorizing the two profiles, he was satisfied he knew all he needed.

'Wait a moment, there's something else here—'

Garcia held up a hand as Carswell rose to leave. He glanced through a flimsy sheet of paper he'd just found inside the package. Then he looked up.

'Do you understand this? It's a general directive from the controller, only it means nothing to me.' Garcia read from the foot of the page, ' "In the event of any eventuality not covered by the enclosed, instruct your operative that war rules will apply." '

'War rules?' Carswell nodded, laughing. 'It's slang, really. There's a whole system of operational methods and procedures they used to teach us back in the resistance days. You know, cut-out points, use of safe houses and so on. Don't worry, Ignacio, they were drummed into us so hard I can remember every single one of them.'

'You British and your rules for playing war—!'

Garcia laughed, shuffled the papers together and put them back into the package.

'All right, so long as you know what you're doing, that's fine by me. Just don't produce a rule which says if anything goes wrong, the local resident gets sent to the wall!'

That was on Saturday. He was in Marseilles now, twenty-four hours later, to sight LeKahn before the mission began. There'd been a photograph attached to the file on Samir, but only a verbal description of the Belgian. Carswell wanted a first-hand visual image before they left so there'd be no identification problem on the road.

He'd been given two addresses for LeKahn. The first turned out to be in a suburb called Vitrolles. It was a shabby, jerry-built district, and Carswell knew as soon as his taxi entered it that there was no chance of his waiting there unobserved. Apart from a few deserted cafés, the only possibility was a bench in one of the blank squares of tarmac and frayed turf which served as the public gardens. There was no café in the Rue Grignan, the street listed for LeKahn, and the nearest garden was several blocks away.

As they drove up the street, Carswell slid down in his seat. LeKahn's house was at the corner of an intersection. It was the same as its neighbours, a tawdry two-storey building with a brown door and the curtains drawn in the ground-floor windows. The brass bell-surround had been polished and someone had planted a row of pink spider-geraniums alongside the gravel path; the straggling flowers, half-flattened by the rain, made a defiant ribbon of colour against the greyness.

As the taxi turned the corner Carswell saw a washing-line above the creosoted fence that hid the back yard; there were women's underclothes hanging from one end of it and a cotton dress fluttered against the pole. LeKahn wasn't married, but he wasn't living alone.

The last thing Carswell noticed was a lean-to garage on the far side of the yard with its swing-door half open. Inside he glimpsed the rear of a scarlet Lancia. It looked new and flamboyant, exactly the sort of car Carswell had imagined the Belgian owning.

Carswell memorized the registration number. Then he leant forward, gave the driver the second address, and they headed back towards the port.

The Rue Caisserie offered infinitely better opportunities for the vantage point he wanted. A hundred yards back from the quays, it was a busy noisy thoroughfare, crowded even on a Sunday afternoon. LeKahn ran his business from a clapboard building halfway along the street. It had probably once been a chandler's or a sailmaker's store and a rusty iron tackle hung above the door. Below it was a newly lettered sign that said AGENCE MONDIALE DE YACHTS ET BATEAUX DIVERS and further down a piece of cardboard had been tacked to the frame with the message that *"ouverture"* was at 9:00 A.M.

Carswell noted a café directly opposite the door. Then he returned to his hotel.

He almost missed LeKahn next morning.

Since Monday was the Belgian's last working day before he

left, Carswell guessed LeKahn would get to his office early. Carswell reached the café at eight, sat down at an outside table and ordered a coffee and croissants.

It was another wet day, with the wind gusting from the sea. There was the same throng of seamen and dockers, the alleyways were blocked with market stalls, and the traffic had been thickened by hundreds of harbour officials cycling to work. Carswell's order arrived and then, as he glanced across the road to see that the door opposite was still locked, he noticed a man shoulder his way along the pavement and stop beneath the iron tackle.

His back was turned but Carswell could see that he was short and powerfully built, with pointed ears and a bald white head. He fiddled with a key, the door opened and he vanished inside. A few moments later he reappeared. He hurried across the street, came into the café and threaded his way between the tables until he was almost at Carswell's shoulder.

Carswell picked up his copy of *Le Sur,* swung round in his chair so that he was facing the glass rain canopy, and lifted the paper to his face.

'Raoul, ça va?'

The voice was light and strangely flat. The café owner replied in a rasping Marseilles accent, and LeKahn gave his order.

'*Deux cartons café et un pain sucré, s'il te plaît.*'

The Belgian half turned towards the street and began to whistle. Carswell could see him reflected in the glass above the rim of the newspaper. He had a pale olive face and a beaked nose with flared nostrils. His eyes were dark and steady. Drops of rain glistened on his head.

He stood there for a moment whistling quietly between his teeth. There was the smell of a damp raincoat mixed with eau de cologne.

Then he swung back towards the counter.

'*Enmerde ce temps, non?*'

'*Casse la tête. Fais trois jours—*'

A paper bag rustled. Carswell saw LeKahn's arm stretch out to take it: broad, stubby, covered with curled black hair at the wrist.

'*Merci, mon vieux.*'

'*Alors, bientôt. Attention aux poulettes!*'

LeKahn ducked under the canopy and ran back across the road. Seconds later Carswell saw him behind one of the first-floor windows. Then he disappeared.

Carswell waited for another quarter of an hour, but there was no further sign of him. In the taxi on the way back to the hotel he analyzed his reaction to the man.

The physical description in the file had been extremely accurate. The squat heavy frame, the bald head and pointed ears, the olive face with its beaked nose and splayed nostrils. Even if he hadn't been able to sight LeKahn before they started, he wouldn't have had the slightest difficulty in picking him out from the written profile alone.

But there'd been something else for which he hadn't been prepared. It had struck him first in the voice, that rapid, colourless, high-pitched sound curiously at odds with the muscular body. Then he'd felt it again when LeKahn swung round whistling and Carswell glimpsed his face in the glass. Everything about LeKahn, his name, his nationality, his record, had prepared Carswell for him to be European.

LeKahn's face wasn't European at all; it was entirely Arab, delicate and fine-boned, with skin as smooth as a woman's.

The rain fell heavily throughout the day, lifted at dusk, then poured down again as darkness came.

Carswell stayed in his room going over the route in front of them. LeKahn would drive first to the Spanish border, then in slow stages south while he carried out the investigations that should result in his finding Samir. Afterwards, he'd presumably head direct for wherever the Arab was hidden.

Carswell's instructions were simply to monitor the Belgian's progress at suitable points, and telephone a report every evening to the operative called Danton. He was also to be particularly alert to the presence of anyone else who appeared to be interested in LeKahn as the journey continued; in the context of the Robespierre serial, that, of course, could mean only the Americans. LeKahn himself would telephone Danton every other evening to give his own report and the next two overnight stopping-places he'd chosen. Calling an hour after the Belgian, Carswell would learn the next phase of the journey.

Since LeKahn wasn't due to make his first contact with Danton until he was well clear of Marseilles, the system wouldn't work on the day they left. It meant that Carswell had to guess where he'd spend Tuesday night.

Carswell decided to solve the problem by taking the night express from Marseilles to Bordeaux and getting out at Narbonne, where the train swung inland. He could hire a car in Narbonne, drive a short distance down the coastal highway to the south and wait until the Lancia passed; it was two months too early for the summer holiday traffic and the brilliant scarlet car would be impossible to miss. Then he could either catch up with it further on or, alternatively, motor straight through to Perpignan, and wait for it again on the far side of the town the next morning.

The Bordeaux express left the main railway station at midnight. Half an hour before it pulled out, Carswell was lying on an upper-berth couchette listening to the rain coursing down the window beside his head.

At five in the morning the sky over Narbonne was a pale violet.

Three hours later, when the Avis booking office opened, Carswell hired a grey Simca and drove along the Mediterranean to a village called Lagrasse. If LeKahn kept to the schedule

Carswell had worked out the day before, the Lancia would pass through Lagrasse between six and seven in the evening.

He spent the day in the village. Then at five he parked the Simca behind one of the two hotels that faced each other across the main street, and walked half a mile out along the coastal highway to a café he'd noticed that morning. It was perched on a bank at a point where the road went through a sharp double-bend below before straightening out on the level stretch that led into Lagrasse.

The front tables commanded two kilometres of the highway as it dropped down a low hill towards the bend. From there he'd be able to spot LeKahn's Lancia cresting the ridge in the distance, follow it down the hill and check it again as it was forced to slow for the corner, before passing directly beneath him.

He sat down and ordered a jug of coffee. It was almost half past five. If he'd guessed correctly, LeKahn would pass by sometime within the next hour.

At nine Carswell was still waiting. Until eight he'd thought LeKahn's departure must have been delayed. But with each ten minutes since he'd become more puzzled. There was no other route the Belgian could have taken and Carswell couldn't think of any reason for him to be travelling more slowly than he'd calculated. By nine, too, the light was beginning to fade; within half an hour the darkness would reduce any car on the road to an anonymous pair of headlamps.

It was entirely by luck that Carswell spotted the Belgian at all.

At nine-thirty a heavy fish-truck appeared on the crest. It lumbered slowly down to the corner, vanished for a moment and then came into sight again, grinding below him at barely twenty kilometres an hour and trailing a great swathe of leaking oil and water. Carswell leant forward to see what had happened, and noticed a car tucked in behind unable to pass, a black Ford station wagon. As he watched, the Ford swerved out, overtook the truck and accelerated away towards the village.

There were two people inside. One of them, the passenger, was a woman; the other, unmistakably, LeKahn.

The car passed so quickly and the westering sun was so low that Carswell wasn't able to get the registration number. He finished his coffee and set off back to Lagrasse. For some reason LeKahn wasn't using the Lancia, and Carswell was briefly irritated with himself that he hadn't considered the possibility. It was imperative he learned the Ford's number; it was a much commoner and less distinctive car and, without the number, identification would be difficult.

The woman was a different matter. In fact, he wasn't absolutely certain that the passenger was a woman: he'd been concentrating on the figure of LeKahn at the wheel. But he'd had an impression of a tangle of black hair and a pale smudgy face peering through the windscreen. He remembered the clothesline behind the little house in Vitrolles and wondered if LeKahn had brought the woman with him. Then he dismissed the idea. The brief had specifically said LeKahn would be travelling alone; it was more likely a hitch-hiker.

Whatever the explanation, he'd find out when he made his first call to Danton later that evening.

By the time Carswell reached the village it was almost dark. He walked up the main street and was about to cross the road to the hotel where his car was parked when he noticed LeKahn's Ford outside the entrance. He drew back into a doorway and waited. A few minutes later LeKahn appeared, followed by a porter. The Belgian unlocked the trunk, stood by the porter while he lifted out two suitcases, closed it again and went back inside.

Carswell thought for a moment. He'd expected LeKahn to spend the first night a couple of hours closer to the Spanish border, but the Belgian had evidently chosen Lagrasse. It left

Carswell with two options: to motor on and pick up the Ford as it came by next day or to spend the night in the village and travel behind LeKahn after they started again. Since his call to Danton was due in an hour, he decided in favour of Lagrasse.

He walked back, crossed the street and worked his way round to the rear of the parking-lot. The Ford had already been moved inside; it was standing near an arch only a few cars away from the Simca. Carswell got into the Simca and drove round to an identical parking-lot behind the other hotel, which faced LeKahn's across the road.

The hotel was almost empty and he was given the room he asked for, overlooking the street on the second floor. He sent the concierge up ahead to draw the curtains. Then he went up himself. He locked the door behind him, turned off the lights and walked to the window.

LeKahn's room was immediately opposite his on the floor below. The evening was still and warm and the curtains were only partly drawn. For several minutes there was nothing except a stretch of wooden floor and a double-bed against the far wall. Then a woman came into the oblong of light.

At first she stood with her back to the window and all Carswell could see was that she was tall and thin with untidy black hair. In fact she was more of a girl than a woman. He realized that when she turned, opened a case on the bed and started to unpack with her face towards him. It was a sulky, knowing slum-child's face, the nose snub, the mouth slashed with lipstick and the eyes hidden in great circles of green and black make-up.

Carswell watched as she took the clothes from the case and stuffed them into the drawers of a bedside table. She couldn't have been more than twenty. She was wearing silver-studded jeans, a loose chiffon blouse and pink platform shoes with cork soles six centimetres high. From the disinterest with which she pulled out LeKahn's shirts, she was obviously no casual pick-up on the road. Presumably, she was the girl from the house in Vitrolles. She might have been anything from a local shop-girl to a young back-street whore.

On the basis of LeKahn's file, Carswell decided she was probably a whore.

As she finished unpacking, LeKahn joined her in the oblong of light. He had a towel knotted round his waist and his shoulders were flecked with water. Naked, he was even more powerful than he'd appeared dressed. Belts of muscle twisted across his back and his stomach was covered with the same dark curling hair Carswell had noticed on his wrists.

He rummaged for a shirt, tugged one out and held it up towards the light, peering at it closely.

'*Minette—*'

The word carried clearly across the street in the still night air. The girl had disappeared and LeKahn was looking across the room at a point hidden by the wall.

'*Quoi?*'

'*Viens ici!*'

'*Qu'est tu veux? Suis occupé—*'

The girl's voice, muffled by the walls, had been sullen and off-hand. Then she wandered back holding something in her hand.

'*Regardes, ma chemise—*'

LeKahn held the shirt out towards her. She glanced down at it, touched the collar and shrugged indifferently.

As she did so LeKahn suddenly hit her. He did it twice, using the flat of his hand and striking her, not on the face, but with rapid chopping movements against her neck. The sound echoed across the street and the girl gulped for air, lifting her head with her mouth distended.

Before she could make any noise LeKahn raised his hand again, holding it close to her face. He paused, standing quite still and staring at her expressionlessly. Then he made a quick beckoning movement towards the bed. The girl closed her mouth and began to undress.

Without her clothes she looked almost beautiful. She kicked away her jeans, glanced at LeKahn, then turned and lay face down on the bed. LeKahn unknotted the towel and dropped on top of her.

A few minutes later he was standing up again rubbing himself briskly. The girl had disappeared once more. It had been a silent functional performance that seemed to have left both of them unmoved; LeKahn had taken her, used her like a piece of cloth and tossed her aside.

'*La prochaine fois, Minette, je t'assure—*'

Carswell let the curtains fall back, walked to the centre of the room and lit a cigarette.

Half an hour afterwards he was on the telephone to Lyon. The voice at the other end, Danton's, was young and slightly nervous. Carswell recounted the day's events, passed on the Ford's registration number and described LeKahn's passenger. LeKahn had said nothing about either her or the car when he'd made his call an hour earlier. Presumably he'd brought the girl along as cover on the basis that a couple would be less conspicuous than a single man.

Danton said he'd check with the Belgian when he telephoned again in forty-eight hours, consult London and let Carswell know if there were any fresh instructions as a result of her presence. Then he gave Carswell the next two nights' stopping-places and rang off.

When Carswell put down the telephone, the room opposite was in darkness.

They were up early the next day.

Carswell woke at seven. By the time he'd showered and dressed, they were both sitting above the street on the hotel terrace. It was another warm summer morning with the same violet sky; occasional trucks thundered past, raising eddies of dust in the roadway, but the village itself was silent and as he stood in the shadow of the window-frame, Carswell could hear the shuffle of their feet under the table.

The girl had chosen a chair in the sunlight. She was wearing her studded jeans again and the same platform-soled shoes, but she'd changed her blouse for a flame-red halter-top. The colour went badly with her hair and heavily painted face, but the halter-top showed the line of her shoulders, light and strong and curiously graceful.

LeKahn was sitting back under an arch of bougainvillea; his hands were motionless on the table in front of him and his face had the sheen of a round fish against the darkness of the leaves.

As the waiter brought them coffee a gust of air carried the smell of the grounds to Carswell's face. He leant against the frame, hidden by the folds of the curtain, and watched.

The girl had an unchanging expression of sullen boredom; LeKahn was merely impassive, a squat white shape sipping his coffee in the shadows. Neither of them spoke except when LeKahn called the waiter again and ordered a glass of anis. He drank it at a single gulp. Then he wiped his mouth delicately, not with a napkin, but with the tips of his fingers like a cat cleaning its face. Fifteen minutes later Carswell saw the black Ford pull away down the street towards Perpignan.

He glanced at his watch; it was exactly nine. They had the Spanish border to cross that day but Gerona, LeKahn's destination for the night, was less than a hundred and fifty miles away.

He went downstairs, had a leisurely breakfast and set off behind them in the Simca.

Carswell followed them for a further five days.

After the first day the routine never varied. LeKahn would leave at nine, driving slowly and keeping to the main roads between the points he'd given Danton. Carswell would set out sometime later, overtake the Ford by a different route, wait for it to come through and then motor on again, overtaking it once more, until he reached the night's stopping-place.

He had no idea what LeKahn did during the parts of the day when the Belgian was out of his sight. The brief had said he'd start by concentrating his inquiries in the north, where he had several possible leads. Since they'd crossed the border they'd never been more than a hundred miles from Barcelona—twice doubling back to one of the Costa Brava resort towns.

On the fourth evening Carswell asked Danton, by now speaking from Saragossa, whether LeKahn had made any progress. Danton said the mission was proceeding satisfactorily but hadn't yet produced anything positive. (Two evenings earlier LeKahn had confirmed the girl was travelling with him as cover; he'd referred to her as a "friend" who knew nothing about what he was doing, and Danton had told Carswell to continue as before.)

There was no sign of anyone else being interested in them. After LeKahn left each morning, Carswell would go into the lobby of his hotel and sit near the desk for half an hour in case anyone asked questions about him. Once he drove back the following day, found the manager and explained he was a friend of LeKahn's who'd been hoping to catch up with him and another group of friends: had anyone else been asking about the Belgian?

The manager shook his head; the hotel was very quiet, there'd been few guests that week and he was certain no one else had enquired after LeKahn.

Every evening Carswell would telephone Saragossa but there was nothing to report.

Over those six days he learned a considerable amount about the Belgian. The man was fastidiously regular in his habits. Breakfast was always at eight o'clock, the girl yawning and heavy-eyed as if she resented being up that early; LeKahn would drink his single cup of coffee and finish with a glass of anis, wiping his mouth with the neat gesture Carswell had witnessed the first morning.

When they passed him during the day—Carswell would wait for them in a bar or café on the highway—LeKahn would be sitting stiffly behind the driving-wheel, gripping it with both hands and staring fixedly ahead. Every evening they both retired to their room for half an hour just after dusk, to carry out, Carswell guessed, that perfunctory sexual exercise he'd watched through the open window. Then they'd eat in the hotel—they never ventured out to a restaurant—and promptly at eleven their bedroom light would be extinguished.

Once or twice he saw LeKahn smile, a slow private smile that momentarily lit up his olive face. Then he'd look almost friendly. The rest of the time he was utterly impassive. The girl never smiled once. Apart from her function to provide a degree of cover, Carswell couldn't understand why LeKahn had brought her with him. He ignored her presence, often not even bothering to answer when she spoke and treating her as if she were a piece of luggage.

The whole journey had a stately, ritual quality to it. More than once Carswell felt the sense of puzzlement he'd felt when he first saw LeKahn's face. There was something incongruous in a mission of assassination which proceeded as leisurely as this one.

The feeling always went quickly. After a lifetime in espionage and counterintelligence, Carswell had long since learned not to question his instructions. The reason had nothing to do with any sense of blind obedience towards his superiors or the Service itself. It lay in the very nature of espionage.

Missions like the Robespierre serial were a matter of patterns, of apparently unrelated functions, disconnected pieces of information, inconsistent activities. The whole pattern, its shape and construction and purpose, was only visible to the person who'd created it—in this case, Carswell guessed, one of the controllers in the building behind Baker Street he'd last visited twelve years ago.

For those like himself who worked in the field it was a matter of trust. Trust that the pattern had been properly drawn. Trust that all the seemingly disparate and conflicting elements fitted together. Trust that provision had been made for any contingency which threatened to force the pattern into a different design.

Carswell also had what were known as the "rules" to fall back on if necessary, the complex system of procedures and initiatives and responses which came into action if an emergency occurred. In the case of the Robespierre serial, the nature of those rules was quite clear. The package from London had specifically stated that the war rules applied.

It meant that when, on Monday, a week after they'd left Marseilles, everything suddenly changed, Carswell knew precisely what to do.

6

Guadalajara

The first part of the day was no different from any other during the week.

LeKahn spent the night near Barcelona. Carswell watched the black Ford leave at nine, checked it again in the early afternoon as it drove south through Tarragona, and then drove on himself to the night's stopping-point, Vinaroz, a village on the main road further south still.

He'd just parked his car and was walking up the main street towards the pension he'd chosen when he saw the Ford brake sharply at a red light ahead. Carswell stopped and turned to face a cigarette kiosk on his left. The lights changed, he heard the hum of an accelerating engine and a moment later the Ford passed behind him. It was travelling much faster than before, and instead of stopping at the square, it continued straight through the village.

It took Carswell half an hour to catch up with them. By then the traffic on the road was thick with home-going trucks and motor-scooters. They'd only made a further forty kilometres when LeKahn swung off the highway and parked in front of a motel. It was seven o'clock; whatever had happened to make him depart from the overnight stopping schedule he'd scrupulously followed all week, it was obvious the Belgian wasn't going to vary his personal travelling arrangements.

Carswell waited beyond the motel until he was certain that they had indeed stopped for the night. Then he drove on to the next village, found a restaurant overlooking the highway, and stayed there until it was time for him to telephone Saragossa.

It took Danton several minutes to understand what Carswell was telling him.

Then he said, 'Wait a moment while I have a look at the map.'

Carswell heard the rustle of paper as Danton searched for Vinaroz.

'Well, I mean, it's only about fifty miles beyond where he said. It's on the same road too, isn't it? He probably just made a small mistake when he spoke to me yesterday.'

'It's possible,' Carswell said, 'but I doubt it. Until this evening he's been absolutely consistent in doing everything he's told you.'

'I think you'd better call me again in a couple of hours. I'll check with London meanwhile. If there has been any development, that'll give him extra time to call through and tell me.'

At midnight Carswell telephoned Saragossa again. There'd been nothing from LeKahn in the meantime, but Danton had relayed Carswell's news to London. London's view was the same as Danton's, and Carswell could hear relief mingled with a certain pomposity in the voice as Danton passed it on.

If anything significant had happened, LeKahn would have interrupted the forty-eight-hour pattern of his calls and rung through to report it. He was still on the coastal highway and only a short distance beyond where he'd said he'd stop. Carswell was to continue as before; he had the following night's destination and they'd be able to find out what had happened when LeKahn telephoned then.

Carswell went back to his table by the restaurant window. Looking at a road map in Baker Street it might well seem that LeKahn had simply made a small error. But after following him for a week on the ground, learning his habits, watching how he behaved, Carswell knew it wasn't in the Belgian's nature to make mistakes.

Something had happened, something important enough to cause him to break his carefully regulated routine.

The second development took place next morning.

Carswell was up at six and ready beside the road half an hour later. He waited there until nine, when the Ford, punctually as always, pulled out of the courtyard and passed him heading south. He let them drive a mile down the road. Then he set off behind.

The traffic was worse than at any time since they'd left Marseilles. Huge diesel trucks, on the run between Barcelona and Valencia, stretched out in unbroken columns for miles in either direction, grinding down to walking pace each time they came to one of the shallow hills that punctuated the highway. Often Carswell would lose sight of the Ford for fifteen minutes, only to see it nudge out round some towering lorry immediately in front, where it must have been crawling along since he'd glimpsed it last.

By midday, three hours after they'd left, they'd travelled less than seventy miles. Then, as he pulled out to overtake an oil truck, Carswell saw that the Ford had stopped on the verge. He passed it quickly and caught sight of LeKahn peering at a map spread over the driving-wheel.

Carswell drove round the next bend and pulled to the side. He waited until there was a tiny gap in the stream of trucks, accelerated sharply amid an angry volley of hooting and managed to make a U turn. He was now facing in the direction from which they'd come. A couple of minutes later, when he heard a second outburst of hooting somewhere ahead of him, he knew his guess was right.

Wherever LeKahn was heading, he'd obviously decided to find another route to it. It was a further ten minutes before

Carswell saw the Ford again. When he did, it was also travelling back towards Vinaroz.

This time they didn't enter the village. A few miles short of it LeKahn turned left up a road that led away from the coast. It was three o'clock. For the next four hours the Ford climbed steadily towards the west through the foothills of the Guadalajara mountains. By seven, when LeKahn pulled up, they were deep in the hill country of Teruel. Well before then Carswell realized there could never have been any question of this being merely a detour to avoid the coastal traffic: whatever LeKahn's final destination, the prearranged stopping-places no longer mattered.

Carswell had already noticed the village in front of him, the first they'd seen in an hour, a huddle of white houses and ochre roofs against the smoke-blue ridges of the mountains beyond. He glanced at his watch, slowed down, parked the Simca off the road under a clump of trees and walked forward.

The road crossed a small ravine and the village started on the far side. There was a single street and the Ford was standing halfway up it outside a two-storey building. As he watched, LeKahn appeared in the doorway, lifted the two cases from the trunk and went inside again. The building was a posada—it had the "P" of the ancient Spanish coaching inns engraved on tiles above the door—and beyond it Carswell could see wires converging on a little telephone exchange.

He glanced up the ravine. There was a stream at its bottom walled with thick dark-green oleander bushes. On the far bank another track, dusty-white in patches between the trees, ran down to join the village somewhere near the exchange. The point where the track came out into the street was hidden by the houses, but there were some café tables on the pavement at the junction.

Carswell crossed the road, climbed down into the ravine and began to walk upstream. His plan was to ford the river a hundred yards up from the road and then walk down the track on the far bank as if he'd come into the village from the other side.

He saw the men as he reached the edge of the second track.

His soft-soled shoes had made no sound as he climbed a ledge of rock above the water. He pushed his way through the oleanders, stepped forward onto the thick powdery surface and stopped. There were three of them, with their backs turned to him. Carswell pressed himself into the bushes and knelt down.

One, in a green shirt, was obviously a Spaniard; both the others looked like Americans. There was no doubt about the tallest of the three, a lean, sorrel-haired man with rimless glasses. The second was much shorter, stocky and heavily muscled, with dark skin and black hair. He was interrogating the Spaniard and from time to time he'd explain something to his tall companion. Carswell caught sight of his face, broad and flat, with slanting eyes, and guessed he was a Filipino.

After a few minutes the Spaniard walked back to the village. The others spoke together for a while. Then they sat down on a boulder near a large Fiat parked under the trees.

Carswell climbed down into the stream-bed again, walked a further fifty yards up the bank and lit a cigarette.

Somehow the CIA had picked up LeKahn's trail just as the brief from London had warned him they might. It was impossible to tell how they'd done it or when they'd got onto him. Carswell was certain no one had followed them along the coast, at least until they'd reached Vinaroz; after that the traffic had been so heavy that countersurveillance would have been impossible, even if his entire attention hadn't been concentrated on tracking the Ford among the columns of trucks.

For the moment it didn't matter how or why they came to be there. All that mattered was to get the news through to Danton on time and to do it without letting any of them, LeKahn or the other three, know of his presence.

By then it was ten to eight. The light was already grey and the high mountain air was crisp with the coming darkness. He crossed the stream again, moved the Simca further back into the trees and walked into the village along the road.

A single street carried the road through two lines of small white-washed houses; there were a few shops, the posada on the right, the café twenty yards beyond it on the left and the telephone exchange further away. The lights were flickering on in the dusk, the pavements were crowded for the evening *paseo,* and the café tables were full of groups of *campesinos,* drinking and playing draughts after the day's work in the forests. Carswell couldn't see the Spaniard in the green shirt, but he must be sitting back near the wall.

The Ford was still parked outside the posada entrance and light was shining from one of the first-floor windows. Thirty yards before it, Carswell stopped and looked round. Apart from the café, there didn't seem to be any other suitable place to watch the posada door. Then an old woman in deep serge-black appeared from the house in front. When she turned to look at him, her puckered walnut-coloured face was watchful but friendly.

Carswell stepped forward and greeted her. He explained he'd been fishing the hill streams and had left his car several miles away over the ridge, and asked if she'd rent him a room for the night so that he could walk back in the morning to collect it. Ten minutes afterwards Carswell was standing in a little stone-floored bedroom with a narrow window over the street. He shut the door, swung himself up onto the sill and settled down to wait; he had a perfect view of the posada and by craning forward he could just see the café tables.

Over the next hour he saw LeKahn three times. Each time he came out of the posada accompanied by a thin melancholy man in a dark suit, probably the manager. They walked up the street to the telephone exchange, vanished inside and then reappeared, the manager shrugging and shaking his head.

LeKahn was obviously having difficulty with his call to Danton and had taken the man with him to translate.

The third time they tried and failed was just after ten. By then it was completely dark and the pavements were deserted, although Carswell could still hear voices and laughter from the café. He lit a cigarette and swore. Until LeKahn got through, there was no point in his telephoning. The Americans' arrival was only one of the two major developments over the past twenty-four hours. The other was LeKahn's sudden and now unquestionable departure from his route. Until London had analyzed the implications of the first and received LeKahn's explanation for the second, Danton wouldn't be able to give him any new instructions.

Carswell leant back against the window-frame and prepared for another wait; LeKahn was trying his call every half hour and it would be ten-thirty before he attempted it again.

A moment later Carswell stiffened and sat forward. A man had appeared from the direction of the café and was walking quickly towards the posada entrance. It was the Filipino. He reached the flight of wooden steps that led up to the door, ran up them and vanished inside.

Instantly, Carswell got down from the sill. He went outside, crossed the road and began to walk cautiously along the pavement towards the pool of light from the posada's ground-floor window. Until then he'd assumed that the three would merely keep the posada under surveillance and follow LeKahn when he left the next morning. Now it was obvious they'd got something else in mind.

The shot sounded when he was less than ten yards from the lighted window.

It was a hollow muffled sound, more of a thump than the sharp crack of a revolver, but Carswell recognized it instantly: a bullet from a low-velocity hand-gun fitted with a compressed-air silencer. As he pressed himself back against the wall he heard the noise twice again. Across the road a couple of *campesinos* hesitated, looked up briefly, then shrugged and walked on; no one at the tables in the café stirred. To anyone who didn't know it, the noise would have been little different from a slammed door.

Then a shadow bisected the lighted roadway, motionless for an instant on the pale earth before wavering away to the right. It was the Filipino. He trotted down the steps, crossed the street and disappeared into the darkness beyond the café. As soon as he'd gone, another figure, the Spaniard, rose from a table at the back and followed him. There was no sign of the sorrel-haired man with the rimless glasses.

Carswell waited a few seconds longer. There'd been no screams from the girl, no shouting from the manager, nothing; just the three shots and the scuff of the Filipino's footsteps as he walked away. He glanced round. There was no one on his side of the street and the conversation in the café continued uninterrupted. Carswell bent down, ran across the few yards that separated him from the doorway, climbed the steps and ducked inside.

The small hall in front was empty and there was no one in the bar through an arch to his right. Immediately ahead a stone staircase led up to the first floor. Beside it was a counter with a key-board on the wall behind. There were nine numbered key-hooks; the key on the fifth hook was missing. Carswell ran up the stairs and came out onto a landing. He paused. There was no sound in the building, but someone was talking distantly in a patio at the back.

Room five was the second door down on the left. He put his hand gently on the knob, twisted it until the catch was free and pushed the door a few millimetres forward; it wasn't locked. He knelt down, kicked it open, rolled inside and crouched on the floor.

For a moment he thought the room was empty. Then he saw LeKahn's foot. It was sticking out behind the end of the bed. He must have been sitting there when the Filipino came in and the shots had knocked him backwards into the gap below the window. There was no sign of the girl.

Carswell stood up and walked over to LeKahn's body. The first shot had hit him in the centre of the chest. The other two had been fired at close range behind his ear. The Filipino had used lead-alloy-headed bullets, which had disintegrated on impact; there was a great pool of blood and bone-splinters on the floor and the counterpane was stained halfway up the bed.

He bent LeKahn's knee and dragged his foot back so that nothing could be seen of him from the rest of the room. Then, as he was standing up again, a door opened at the end of the corridor. Carswell went back to the inside wall and flattened himself against the door-frame. A moment later the handle turned and the girl came in. Her hair was wet and she was wearing a towelling dressing-gown.

'Jean—'

As she looked round for LeKahn she saw Carswell standing behind her.

She gazed at him for an instant, her face stiffened, then she opened her mouth to scream. Carswell jumped forward, clamped his hand over her mouth and swung her round with her arm twisted up behind her. There was a muffled grunt, she wriggled briefly, then she felt the pain of the arm-lock and stopped, tense and shivering in front of him.

'Listen to me—'

Carswell spoke rapidly and quietly in French.

'Listen very carefully. Jean's dead, he's been killed. He's over there in the corner by the bed—'

He forced her across the floor until she could see LeKahn's legs, but kept her far enough away so that his head was hidden. As he pulled her back into the middle of the room, her eyes widened and her mouth twitched under his palm.

'No, it wasn't me.' Carswell shook his head hard. 'It happened a few minutes ago, just before I got here. If it had been me, I'd have left immediately or I'd have killed you too by now. Do you understand?'

She gazed at him for a moment, her head twisted round and her face terrified. Then she relaxed slightly and nodded.

'Good. And if I take my hand away, will you be absolutely quiet? Because although I didn't touch Jean, I promise I will kill you if you make the slightest sound.'

He removed his hand as she nodded again. She rubbed her lips, white from the pressure of his palm. Then she glanced at the bed.

'What happened? He was sitting there reading the paper when I went for a shower. Why—?'

The words were mumbled and she was still trembling, but she was calmer than a moment ago.

'You're called Minette, aren't you?'

'Yes.' Her eyes narrowed. 'How did you know?'

'Because I've been following you and I heard Jean calling you that. I was sent by the same people who employed Jean. He didn't know I was with you, but I was—ever since you left Marseilles. Did you know what Jean was doing?'

She shook her head. 'He wasn't doing anything. We were on a holiday—'

'No, Minette,' Carswell cut her off, 'Jean wasn't on holiday. I don't know what he told you, but he was working, doing something extremely dangerous. That's why he was killed. Now I want you to come with me—'

As he finished, she opened her mouth again and looked as if she was about to scream. He caught hold of her and jammed his hand back over her face.

'Minette, the men who killed Jean are still here in the village. They may come back, they may be after you, too. Do you realize that? And even if they don't, you'll be found here alone with Jean's body. No, you didn't kill him but the police won't know that. And even if they believe you in the end, they'll keep you for weeks, maybe months, in prison—'

She had gone limp and Carswell thought she was going to

faint. But she recovered and started to cry, the tears rolling silently down her cheeks while her body shook.

The door hadn't closed properly after she'd come in. Through the crack he could hear the voice in the rear patio, louder now, as if calling for someone.

'Apart from being in danger, you're in very serious trouble, Minette.' Carswell had taken his hand from her mouth again. 'Now, are you going to come with me, or am I going to leave you here on your own?'

'I'll come.' The words came out slowly between the sobs. 'Who are you?'

'A friend of Jean's.' He heard the voice in the patio again. 'I'll explain later. Get dressed.'

She looked at him for a moment. Then she took off her dressing-gown and stood naked searching for some clothes. She put on her jeans and a shirt and reached for the platform-soled shoes she'd worn all week. Carswell told her to change them for a less cumbersome pair and made her find a sweater.

While she was looking, he opened a case lying on the floor by the bed. It was LeKahn's and it was still unpacked. The object he was after was wrapped in a dirty towel at the bottom, a heavy rectangular box about two feet long and fitted with a Yale lock. He lifted it out, tucked it under his arm and went to the door.

Apart from the same distant voice, there was still no sound outside. He turned off the light, took the girl's hand, locked the door behind them and set off along the corridor. They reached the stairs and started down. As Carswell's foot touched the last step, the head and shoulders of the manager suddenly appeared round the arch into the bar.

Carswell froze, his fingernails cutting into the girl's palm. The manager was pulling something behind him, a crate of bottles which bumped over the stone-flagged floor. For a moment it looked as if he'd cross the hall and disappear behind the counter without seeing them. Then he paused, rubbed his back and looked up yawning.

Carswell let go of the girl, rocked forward and hit him, immediately and instinctively, with the edge of his hand. It was a massive blow, coming from above and catching the man at the base of his neck, and he crumpled soundlessly to the ground.

Behind Carswell the girl sobbed again, a shocked half-choked sound.

'Go out and get into the passenger seat of Jean's car. Shut the door quietly and wait for me. I'll join you in a moment.'

He watched her until she was sitting inside with the door closed. Then he bent down and looked at the man. He must have died the instant Carswell hit him; his head was wrenched out at an angle to his shoulders and his mouth was still open. The creases on the worn shiny cloth of his suit had been carefully pressed and the light was glittering on a little St. Christopher medallion on his lapel.

Carswell shut his eyes; he felt sick and the tendons of his wrists were quivering. He shook his head, looked up and noticed a cupboard under the stairs. The manager must have been dragging the crate towards it when they came down; the door was open and a heavy padlock was hanging from the bolt. Carswell dragged the body inside, closed the door and snapped the padlock shut.

He went outside, started the Ford, reversed it into a parking space beside the posada and drove out along the road by which he'd entered the village two hours earlier. He was sweating and there was a sour dry taste in his throat. A few heads looked up from the café as the car disappeared, but that was all.

Five minutes later he turned off the road, bumped down through the trees and stopped beside the Simca. The girl hadn't spoken since they'd left.

Carswell opened his door and said, 'I'll be another few minutes. Don't move until I come back.'

He walked over to the Simca, pulled out the road-map and studied it by the wavering flame of his lighter. Then he lit a cigarette and inhaled deeply.

By now the Americans would be well on their way back to Madrid. So far they'd had considerable luck. Unless a woodman had noticed their car on the track, he doubted whether anyone in the village would even remember seeing them. They'd have nothing to worry about until they read the newspaper reports of what had happened. Then they'd have to work out how there came to be another body in the posada and what had happened to the girl. The obvious assumption was that LeKahn hadn't been working alone. That realization wouldn't help them now: however they'd traced the Belgian, they clearly didn't know about Carswell—or they'd already have taken the same action against him.

It meant he had at least two days before they could even guess his existence. By then he could have disappeared so completely that they'd have no chance of finding him—at least not before the deadline for the end of the mission was past. Whether there was any mission now left to complete depended on the answer to one crucial question: Had LeKahn somehow discovered where Samir was hidden?

Carswell was virtually certain he had. The Belgian was too experienced, too consistent, too much a creature of professional habit to have broken the pattern for anything else. If Carswell was right, it would explain everything: the increased speed, the abrupt change in the route, the bypassing of the prearranged stopping-places.

There was only one person who could provide the answer now: the girl.

Meanwhile, he had the Spanish police to contend with. Normally, there'd have been little chance of LeKahn's body being discovered before morning. With the light out and the door locked, any passing maid would assume the couple inside were asleep. The problem was the manager. Yet with luck he too wouldn't be missed until next day; since LeKahn's car had gone from the street, it might be assumed he'd accompanied the Belgian on a search for another telephone.

Nothing would happen for two hours at least. Even then it would be the following morning before a full police hunt could be launched. There was probably only a pair of *guardia civil* in the village. By the time a criminal investigation unit had arrived, the villagers had been questioned, and descriptions obtained of himself, the girl and the Ford, it would be midday at the earliest.

Providing he got away from the immediate area in the Simca, which it was doubtful anyone had seen, he could reasonably count on having the night in which to move freely. Afterwards, he'd inevitably be the prime suspect; the old woman's description, however vague and fragmentary, would see to that.

By then it might not matter anyway. If the girl didn't know where LeKahn was heading, he'd be safely back in Madrid, with nothing to link him to the unexplained murders of a Belgian and a posada manager in the Guadalajara mountains.

Carswell stood up and walked back to the Ford. The girl was gazing into the darkness. While he'd been away she'd made up her face. Now she was crying. The tears had cut deep runnels through the thick cream and powder; in the moonlight they looked like razor-scars.

'Minette—'

As Carswell bent down, a wave of scent came through the window.

'When are we going back to Marseilles?' she said.

'Quite soon. But before we do, there's something I need to know—'

'I want to go back to Marseilles.' She didn't look at him, she simply sat staring through the windscreen. 'Please drive me back to Marseilles. Please do it now.'

She'd stopped crying and her voice was very calm, as if she'd been rehearsing the words.

'I will help you, Minette. But listen first—'

'*You* listen to me! You—*salaud!*'

Her hand came out before Carswell realized what was happening. There was the flash of something white in the darkness and the dragging pain of her nails on his cheek.

He jerked back, hitting his head against the window-frame, and put a hand up to his face. He could feel the blood trickling out between his fingers. He reached into his pocket for a handkerchief, rolled it into a ball and pressed it against his skin.

'I don't know who you are, I don't know what you're doing—'

She hadn't started to cry again but she was breathing quickly and her face was taut.

'Maybe you did kill Jean, I just don't care. But you got me out here; you said I was in trouble, and you'd help. Well, all the help I want is to get back to Marseilles. No talking, no listening, no questions, nothing. Do you understand? Fuck you, nothing!'

Her hand was still lying clenched on the door. Carswell waited a moment. Then he grabbed at her wrist. She struggled violently, heaving herself backwards and forwards in the seat and trying to lower her head so that she could sink her teeth into his arm.

Her attack had been so fast and unexpected that Carswell hadn't even felt angry until then. Now, with the blood running into his mouth and his cheek aching, he twisted her wrist and levered it sharply upwards.

'If you don't stop that, Minette, I'll break your bloody arm right now. I mean it.'

For another minute she fought against him, before she suddenly went limp and slumped back.

'What the hell do you want?'

Keeping his eyes on her face, Carswell slowly relaxed his grip.

'I want to know where you were going,' he said.

'Going? What do you mean?' She shrugged. 'We weren't going anywhere. I told you, a holiday—'

'You may have thought so, but Jean wasn't. I was working with him; that's why I was following you—'

She looked at him sullenly and suspiciously.

'Jean was looking for someone, Minette. I think he found where that person was and he told you. That's what I want to know.'

'You think I'd tell you anything, you little bastard!'

'Fine, I don't mind. You've got the keys of the car. The police won't be looking for it for at least an hour yet—'

Carswell turned towards the Simca.

'That won't quite give you time to make the French border, but you can probably walk the last few hundred kilometres. And even if they do catch up with you first, I'm sure you'll be able to explain everything—Jean's body, running away, all the rest of it.'

He'd opened the car door and was starting to get inside before she spoke again.

'We were just driving. Nowhere in particular, or Jean never told me, anyway. We used to start in the morning, sometimes he'd say where we'd stop that night, other times we'd just arrive and he'd say "All right, we'll stay here." That's true. Honest.'

The defiance had gone and her voice sounded weary and indifferent. Carswell walked back to the Ford.

'Did he say where you were going to stay tomorrow?'

'No.'

'Today you left the coast—'

In the distance Carswell heard the hum of a motor-scooter. He broke off, turned towards the trees that lined the road and saw the gleam of a lamp. It wavered away towards the village and the engine noise faded.

'Get your things, Minette.' He glanced back at her. 'We're going for a drive.'

'Why?'

'Because it's too dangerous to stay here. Come on, get out.'

She picked up her sweater and make-up case and climbed out of the Ford. Standing upright beside it she was almost as tall as he was.

'Where are we going?'

'To find somewhere we can talk.'

'I can't fucking tell you what I don't know, can I?'

Carswell shook his head. 'If I'm right, you do know, Minette. You may not realize it, but you know.'

'*Salaud!*'

As she bent down to get into the Simca she suddenly spat at his face. Carswell rocked back but when he stepped forward to seize her again, she was already sitting inside.

'If you do anything like that again, I'll hit you harder than you've ever been hit.'

He slammed the door, wiped the saliva from his face, went over to the Ford and searched it quickly.

It was another rented car; the papers in the dashboard showed that it had been taken out by M. Emil Anquetil, a commercial traveller from Avignon, who'd hired it fully insured for a month, with cash paid in advance. There was nothing in it apart from a few maps and a leather case containing two bottles of Evian water.

Carswell rubbed down the most obvious surfaces with the windscreen cloth; he hadn't time to do a thorough job and there'd inevitably be some of LeKahn's finger-prints left, but he was fairly certain he got rid of his own. He took off the handbrake and rolled the car into the undergrowth; it wouldn't evade a serious search, but at least it would be invisible from the road.

Finally, he took the Evian water and the bulky package he'd

found in LeKahn's case, returned to the Simca and drove up to the road. Fifteen minutes later he was ten kilometres from the village and heading back in the direction from which they'd come that morning.

The girl hadn't spoken again and Carswell decided not to question her further until he found somewhere to stop when they were well clear of the area. As they turned a corner and began descending into a valley, she lifted her head and glanced across at him.

'I'm saying the truth,' she said.

'Maybe, Minette, maybe you just think you are. Either way, I'm going to find out for sure, even if it takes the whole night.'

'What will you do afterwards?'

'Try to get you on a train or something, get you back to France.' Carswell paused. 'Of course, the sooner I know, the sooner that'll be.'

'Is there a lot of money in it?'

'Money?' Carswell laughed. 'I don't know what it was worth to Jean, but for me it'll be the week's salary for as long as it takes. It's just work, that's all, the same as it might be anyone else's. The people who employed Jean gave him an important job to do. Because I work for them, too, and he's dead now, I'll have to finish the job in his place. It's the way we operate.'

Carswell had barely thought about it until then. From the moment he'd found LeKahn's body his responses had been reflex, unconscious. Even if the London brief hadn't instructed him to follow the war rules, he'd probably still have acted in the same way.

Yet the war rules had been laid down for the operation and the procedure was quite explicit for the situation created by the Belgian's death: if a free-lance agent under surveillance by a covert escort became inoperative for any reason, the escort took over the agent's role and became responsible for completing the mission. Now that LeKahn was dead it was up to

Carswell to finish the serial. That meant finding and terminating a man he knew from the profile as a bearded fifty-seven-year-old Arab.

Whether Carswell could find him depended entirely on his belief that LeKahn had discovered the man's hiding-place—and that somehow the girl knew it too. An image of a blue-and-silver St. Christopher medallion hovered momentarily in front of him. Carswell deliberately excised it from his mind, accelerated out of the valley and climbed the hill on the far side.

He had twenty-four hours. In that time he'd either learn he was right—or break the girl in the process.

7

London

Vavasseur telephoned at four-thirty.

It was Friday afternoon, forty-eight hours before LeKahn abruptly changed his route and drove through the village where he'd told Danton he'd spend the night. In the twelve days since the Belgian had left Marseilles on his Middle Eastern trip, the Robespierre serial's coda had followed precisely the pattern Handley-Reid had intended.

The results—the Joint Intelligence community signals which had tracked LeKahn through Beirut and Riyadh and then reported his second departure from Marseilles—were lying in a folder on Handley-Reid's desk. All that remained was for Vavasseur, who'd have drawn his own conclusions from his copies of the same signals, to contact him. He came through within an hour of the time Handley-Reid had predicted.

For a moment his voice, crackling slightly over the scrambled line from Paris, was casual and friendly. Then he came straight to the point.

'I assume the P9 I put through has reached you, Charles?'

'Yes, I got it about twenty minutes ago.'

A "Priority 9" was the highest level and most urgent request for assistance used by the allied intelligence agencies. Vavasseur's P9 had asked for the Service's help in tracing a subject who "may be using one or more aliases but whom you will probably have S-listed under the name Jean LeKahn."

'Good,' Vavasseur said. 'We didn't mince words before, Charles, let's not do it now. You weren't remotely surprised to get a P9 involving your Robespierre identity, were you?'

'No, frankly, I wasn't—'

'Of course you weren't. From the moment you got that first Brussels signal, you've had every one of your sections out there wearing their butts off to find out whether there was anything useful behind it.'

'We took the usual steps.'

'The usual steps?' Vavasseur paused. 'I should tell you, Charles, that my immediate thought when I learned about this Belgian was that he might well be one of your "usual steps" himself.'

There was a brief silence.

'All right,' Vavasseur went on, 'I won't press the point. I honestly don't care whether he's an amateur ornithologist on vacation from your accounts department. I just don't like the idea of him being around. Our little friend's too valuable—to both of us—for speculation.'

'To both of us?'

'That's what I said.'

Briefly, Handley-Reid heard an edge of irritation in Vavasseur's voice.

'I've already spoken to Langley. Providing you can find this LeKahn for us before he tries anything—unwise—then you can tell your Foreign Office they can see the little Arab as soon as they want. You'll have that confirmed direct from Washington today.'

'I can't make any promises, of course.'

'I'm not remotely interested in promises, Charles.' The irritation sounded again. 'I'll be quite blunt about it: to my mind the whole thing stinks. But I'm not prepared to take any chances. So if your much-vaunted sections out there can come up with the answer, you've got us over a barrel. If not, then you're out of the ball game.'

'I'll come back to you as soon as I've got any news.'

Handley-Reid waited twenty-four hours. Then late on Saturday evening he called Vavasseur back.

'Well, we've had a certain amount of luck,' Handley-Reid said.

'You amaze me, Charles.'

'LeKahn was approached some time round May 4 by members of a group called Al Wahzan. He'd dealt with them before over an arms shipment through Benghazi—'

Handley-Reid went through the scenario that Mather had prepared to explain how and when LeKahn had been given the contract to kill Samir.

'He left Marseilles for the second time on May 15—'

'We know that,' Vavasseur cut in. 'What interests me is what he did then and where he is now.'

'He drove to the border and crossed into Spain. Our sources are vaguer on whether he actually knows where you've put Samir. You can probably deduce that from his movements.'

'Whatever I deduce from his movements, I need to know first where he's moving from.'

'Well, again I can't be specific,' Handley-Reid said. 'But I think I can get you close enough. He's travelling by car, heading south down the coastal highway. The car's a black Ford station wagon with this registration number—'

Handley-Reid glanced at his note pad and read out the number which Carswell had telephoned through to Spencer five days earlier.

'LeKahn spent last night at a place called Sitges. By tomorrow he should be about a hundred and fifty miles further south.'

He waited while Vavasseur wrote down the details. Then he heard Vavasseur's voice again.

'Your crystal ball must really be working overtime, Charles!'

'Oh, it's not magic. I wish it was!' Handley-Reid laughed. 'Al Wahzan hired the car for him; one of our people was prudent enough to ask to see the receipt—reasonably, I think, in view of what we paid for the information. And he called Beirut last night; we don't know what he said but we did learn where he was speaking from. It's as simple as that.'

'I doubt it, Charles, I really doubt it.' Vavasseur was as bland as at the start. 'But I'll leave it there for the moment. One day we'll have a long drink together, you and I, and you can tell me what truly happened.'

Handley-Reid smiled. 'Meanwhile, can I assume we've earned our money?'

'You've certainly earned your access to the little man, if that's what you mean, or you will have just as soon as we catch up with this Belgian ornithologist tomorrow.'

Handley-Reid put down the telephone. Just before he went out he glanced at the window. For the first time in a month the rain had stopped and the sky was bright with stars. He could telephone Spencer in the morning and tell him to send LeKahn's escort back to Madrid when he made his routine call that evening.

Handley-Reid shut the door. The Robespierre serial was over.

8

Teruel

It was eleven when Carswell and the girl set off down the road they'd driven up separately that afternoon.

The night was clear and windless, with a full moon curving westwards overhead. Once a fox appeared on the road in front of them, running straight and fast before the headlamps like a travelling plume of red-brown dust. Occasional owls coasted down in the beams and small mountain moths shone briefly in brilliant white constellations as the car passed.

Carswell drove for two hours before he found the place he was looking for. By then they'd made a large semi-circle, turning off the original road onto another which led south and later onto a third that ran back west. He'd given up using the map, and used the stars to guide him instead. Now they were travelling roughly parallel to the first road; the village where LeKahn had been killed was twenty miles across the mountains to the north.

They climbed a steep hill, came out onto a broad ridge and followed it until a large clump of rocks appeared on the left. Carswell slowed down. There were no lights in the surrounding darkness and they hadn't passed another vehicle since they'd started. He turned off the road, bumped down a shallow sandy ravine and came to a halt in the lee of a huge boulder.

'Stay here.'

The girl didn't bother to respond as he got out and walked round the boulder.

On the far side was a small clearing walled by the rocks. From its centre he could see the knife-edge crests of mountain peaks. At one end a table of bark, dry reeds and brushwood spilled onto the sand from the mouth of a narrow cleft. The air was cold and patches of frost-crystals shone on the rock-faces.

Carswell picked up an armful of the wood, piled it into a cone and lit a fire. When it was blazing, he climbed over the wall of rock and walked round the clump. The flames were invisible from the road and from the two flanks; the only place from which they might be seen was the crest of a ridge above the neighbouring valley. Even if they were, the fire would be taken as the site of some logging camp. The countryside was heavily timbered and there'd been mounds of felled trees every few miles throughout the drive.

He went back to the car and opened the door. The girl was sitting hunched down in her seat with her eyes closed.

'All right, Minette, out you get.'

'I'm cold, and I want to sleep.'

'I've lit a fire. You'll be warmer beside it.'

She glanced at the circle of rocks. Then she looked back at him.

'I just want to sleep here.'

'You don't sleep anywhere until we've talked.'

'You little ponce, fuck you!'

She clenched her hands as if she was about to jump at him again.

'Remember what I said.'

When they reached the clearing, he pulled a log over to the fire and waited until she was seated, holding her hands up to the flames. Then he squatted by her on the sand.

'Minette, I know you're cold and tired and this whole evening's been horrible. I'm sorry about Jean, but neither of us can do anything about that now. What I can do, and I promise you I will, is get you back to Marseilles—'

'Promise! How the Christ do I know you'll do what you promise?'

'You don't, obviously. You'll just have to trust me.'

She leant back on the log and burst into laughter.

'Trust you? Listen, you—what are you called?'

'Jean.'

Carswell had used the French version of the name, and she laughed again.

'Jean! That's lovely, two lying little ponces and you both even have the same name. Oh, that's beautiful! Well, listen, my other little Jean—'

Her mouth dragged down at the corners and she spat the words out between her teeth.

'I know you, you filthy little prick. I've known people same as you all my life. You and the other Jean and all the rest of the Jeans, too. And you did the same as all of them; conned me, conned me into coming with you because you said you'd help. You'll help me, like fuck you will! Yes, I know where Jean was going and I'll tell you. Only we'll do it my way. And that means when we're back in Marseilles—that or nothing!'

She swept her hand out in a flat chopping gesture and stopped.

Carswell said nothing. The whole outburst had been credible, almost convincing: only the claim at the end—that she knew LeKahn's destination—rang untrue.

She didn't know where LeKahn was headed. Carswell was sure of that now. Before, she might have been lying, afraid that if she told him he'd abandon her immediately, perhaps even kill her. Not any longer. The despair and fury in her voice had been too violent to be counterfeited. She believed she'd been fooled into leaving the posada at a moment of terrified confusion; she realized now that she'd compromised herself hopelessly in the eyes of the Spanish police; and she knew too that she'd nothing to barter with Carswell for her return to France.

That at least was what she must have thought. Possibly she was right. Yet something in Carswell refused to accept it; after that week, after the meticulous regularity of the seven days' journey, he couldn't believe that LeKahn had changed the pattern so suddenly and radically without communicating some hint of what had happened.

She may not have known it consciously, but somehow the Belgian must have revealed the reason.

'The way we're going, Minette,' he said finally, 'I rather doubt whether you'll ever see Marseilles again.'

There was silence for a moment.

'All right, so it's not true.' She shrugged. 'I don't know where we were going, I never did. And that is true, I promise you, promise you on the cross and in the name of Mary—if that means anything to you at all!'

The bitterness flared briefly again in her voice.

'So what are you going to do? Christ, why don't you just use that gun on me like you did on Jean? Save time, wouldn't it?'

'Come on, Minette. I didn't kill Jean. You know that. Here—'

Carswell pulled out a pack of cigarettes and offered her one. She shook her head.

'All right.' He lit a cigarette for himself. 'I believe you. But I also believe that if you think back, you'll remember something he said, maybe even something you saw him do. Something that means nothing to you, but may tell me what I want.'

'You're stupid!' She shook her head. 'Look, if I knew anything, anything at all, I'd tell you now. I mean, what have I got to lose? You'll probably kill me anyway. Isn't that about all pricks like you know what to do—?'

She lifted her head as she finished. She'd been yawning

ever since they sat down by the fire and Carswell saw that under the cracked and streaked make-up her face was beginning to sag with tiredness.

'No, I didn't mean that. I could quite fancy you in a way, know what I mean? Christ, at least you haven't hit me yet. Jean would have, that bastard; he'd have broken my nose by now. Poor bald fat Jean lying there all by himself—'

She giggled, put both hands on the log and heaved herself to her feet.

'Good-bye, *petit* fucking Jean, that's what I say! See me talking to him? Christ, you must be joking! But I'll talk to you, promise, anything you want. Let's just sleep a little first. It's warm here by the fire, did you know that, all warm and soft—'

She turned away from him, yawned again and knelt on the sand, scrabbling with her hands as if she was scooping out a trough to make a bed for herself.

'Get up, Minette.'

'I'm going to sleep.'

'No you're not, not yet anyway—'

Carswell was still squatting by the fire watching her impassively. As he reached forward to pull her upright, she suddenly kicked out at him.

Stiff and unbalanced, he was caught completely off guard. The ball of her foot hit him in the groin, he sprawled back, fell into the edge of the fire and rolled away gasping. As he lay there retching, she stood up, grabbed a heavy stone and smashed it down towards his head. Carswell managed to jerk away and levered himself to his feet while she was searching for another.

When she came at him again he chopped her hard in the stomach. She grunted, stumbled back and fell over.

'I warned you, Minette—'

She was crouched on her hands and knees. Carswell lifted her up and hit her five times very quickly across the side of her head, his hand cutting backwards and forwards in a spasm of pain, anger and fatigue. Then he spread out his knuckles and jabbed them at her breasts.

She fell down again screaming, her ears scarlet from the blows and her arms cradled tightly round her chest. Carswell let her lie there for a few seconds. Then he picked her up and pushed her towards the log.

She sat there rocking from side to side sobbing.

'You think Jean could hurt you, Minette? Believe me, he was an amateur. That was nothing I did then, nothing. Next time I'll do things that'll make you wish you'd never been born. And after that, I'll really start. Understand?'

She nodded.

'Right. I'm going to make some coffee—'

He went back to the car, collected his travelling bag and brewed coffee over the fire.

By the time he'd finished, the girl had stopped crying and was sitting shuddering occasionally, her eyes gazing dully into the flames: patches of make-up had been scraped from her face and the skin showed through, reddening and bruised. When he offered her a mug she nodded and began to drink.

'Are we starting to understand each other?'

She nodded again. Then she glanced at him hesitantly. 'I'm cold, really cold.'

'I'll get you a rug.'

Carswell collected a blanket from the car and draped it round her shoulders.

'Is that better?'

'Yes.'

'Good. Well, let's try again, let's go right back to the beginning of this—holiday.'

He sat down by the log. Everything seemed to have drained out of her and she was sitting quite still, the mug cupped in her hands, waiting for him to go on.

'Did Jean say why he was taking it?'

'Not really. Just to enjoy himself, I thought.'

'Nothing else? Nothing about some business he had to do as well?'

'No.'

'But he saw people, didn't he? The other side of Barcelona, you went back there twice. Why was that?'

'I don't know,' she said. 'He left me in a café. Friends, I suppose. He had friends all over. Well, not exactly friends, people he did business with. You know—'

'Did you know anything about his business?'

'Yes, he had the boat thing. Then there was some land somewhere, I can't remember where. Oh, he had all sorts of things.'

'Did he ever talk to you about them?'

'What do you think I was, his partner—?'

She glanced at Carswell scornfully. Until then her answers had been listless. Now life briefly came back into her voice.

'I was there to be screwed, that's all. Oh, to cook and clean and wash, sure, but that's part of it, isn't it? Only, nothing else, nothing fancy like being made love to. Just screwed. Period. And you don't talk business when you're screwing, at least not with Jean, you didn't.'

She shook her head wearily. Carswell waited a moment. Then he tried again.

'Jean had a leather case in his baggage,' he said, 'the one I took with me when we left your room. Do you remember it?'

'Of course I do.'

'Do you know what's inside it?'

'*Merde!* Who do you think I am?'

'But why on this trip, this—holiday?'

'Why did he take his gun?' She laughed. 'You want a reason? Listen, I'll tell you, you give a man like Jean a reason *not* to take his gun anywhere—then you've got a reason. Right?'

'All right, Minette. You were on holiday with a man who carried a gun like other people carry spare tooth-brushes. You drove with him slowly down the east coast of Spain. Then suddenly you changed direction, you headed inland, you started motoring like there was no tomorrow. Why? Well, let's go over it on the map—'

Carswell spread out the road-map in the firelight and began to retrace the route.

Three hours later the darkness was becoming paler. A flock of wood pigeons crested the wall of rock, banked sharply as they saw the embers of the fire and clamoured away over the valley, startled shapes against the sky. Then a blade of light, grey-blue and ribbed with gold, lifted over the furthest mountain ridge, and faintly a distant dog barked.

Carswell put away the map, stood up stiffly and walked to the rim of the clearing. The air was clean and fresh with the coming day. Behind him the girl lurched sideways and hung over the fire, her head sunk on her chest, asleep.

He had got nowhere. They'd covered every single mile of the trip, but she could remember nothing that helped; no stopping-point, no person LeKahn had spoken to, no comment he'd made during the drive or over one of their meals, nothing. As far as she was concerned they'd simply been on a motoring holiday. She hadn't even asked why they'd left the coast. To her it was just one of LeKahn's whims; there might have been another friend he wanted to see, a town he wanted to visit, a road that was less crowded than the highway. She hadn't known and she hadn't cared.

Yet Carswell remained inflexibly convinced, not just that there'd been a reason for the sudden change, a reason that concerned Samir's hiding-place, but that the Belgian must have communicated it to her. Not directly—it would have happened through some hint, some enigmatic remark, some casual thrown-away comment whose significance she hadn't understood.

But that she did know, that the answer lay buried somewhere in her memory, of that he was certain.

He glanced at his watch; it was just before five. He went back to the fire, leant down and shook the girl by the shoulder.

'Come on, Minette—'

Her head lolled to one side; for a moment her bleared eyes opened and she peered up at him. Then she rolled away and tried to settle back into sleep.

Carswell shook her again hard. 'I'm sorry but we're moving on.'

He helped her to her feet and she stumbled alongside him to the car. He went back to the fire. The flames had burned down and all that was left was a smouldering circle of charcoal. He covered it with sand, brushed away their footprints, returned to the Simca and drove up to the road.

It was still dark enough to use the headlamps, but the dawn was coming fast and the trees were stirring with birds.

'Where now?'

The sound of the engine had woken her again and her voice was hoarse.

'Lower into the valleys. It's too exposed up here. We'll find somewhere to hide for the day—'

Her head dropped forward onto her chest and she slid sideways until she was resting against the door.

Carswell glanced at her. Her face was pinched and white in the half-light, and there were black circles under her eyes. He leant across, wound down her window and afterwards did the same with his. The two streams of air were hard and chill and bit sharply at his skin.

She stiffened immediately and sat upright, shivering.

'I'm sorry, Minette, but we're going to talk all the way. And when we get there we'll go on talking. You and I are going to talk until neither of us has any words left—and then we'll use signs. But you're going to tell me what I want to know—and that's a promise.'

9

Teruel

They drove until the sun was over the mountain ridges that rimmed the horizon.

The road was the same as before, a roughly paved track that climbed tortuously up the hills between dense walls of trees, or wound slowly along the valleys below. For the first hour there was no traffic at all, not even a logging cart. Then at half past six they passed a group of woodmen and soon afterwards a baker's van and some trucks. Once a couple of *guardia civil* on motor-scooters went by; they glanced incuriously at the grey Simca, nodded a greeting and disappeared in the opposite direction.

Occasionally they came to a roadside café with *campesinos* eating breakfast at bench-tables in the courtyard outside; coffee, thick red slices of *chorizo*—the dried mountain sausage—and hunks of black bread dipped in olive oil. Carswell could smell the smoke from the clay ovens through the open window and felt the tug of hunger in his stomach. They'd have to buy something to eat later in the day but that would be after he'd abandoned the car.

The village where LeKahn had been killed was still less than fifty miles away. He wanted to get as far from it as possible before he was forced to find some other means of transport. It could only be a few hours now before a full alert was put out—certainly for the girl, who'd be identified first, and then for himself.

Carswell looked across at her. She was hunched forward on the seat. Her arms were wrapped tightly round her against the cold and her mouth was slack, but her eyes were still open.

'So what did you do then?'

'Then—?'

She shook her head, trying to dispel the torpor that had momentarily silenced her.

'Another store, can't remember its name. But they'd heard what happened at Prisunic. So while I was waiting after the interview, they called the police. There was a glass door and I saw them coming up the stairs. So I ran to the toilet and climbed out. Only, then I knew I couldn't stay in Marseilles. So I went to the station—'

In the two hours since they'd left the ridge, Carswell had learned a great deal about the girl.

Her real name was Marie Vercors, although she'd always been known as Minette. She was just nineteen and she'd been born in Berliet, a slum behind the new harbour to the west of Marseilles, where her father worked as a stevedore. He'd walked out on her mother when Minette was three. A couple of years later, after her arm had been broken by the latest in a succession of "stepfathers," she'd been taken into care by the social-welfare authorities.

The next twelve years were predictable; foster-homes, long hours of housework, truancy from school, punishment, petty crime, beatings-up, runnings away, being recaptured like some animal escaped from its cage and returned to further drudgery, further degradation. The whole joyless catalogue of a childhood spent in the hands of people whose sole preoccupation was to patronize, exploit or brutalize any child like Minette over whom they'd temporarily been given power.

Her first real trouble came at fifteen, when she was caught pilfering from a store. She was given a suspended sentence, went to work at another store, stole again and ran away to Toulon. Coming back a year later, when she'd naïvely thought the police would have forgotten about her, she was arrested within a week and sent to a juvenile prison. A month after she was released, she'd taken up with a Corsican and was a fifty-franc whore in the docks.

LeKahn had seen her there one evening. Fifty-franc waterfront prostitutes weren't his usual choice, but there must have been something about the girl which attracted him. He picked her up and instead of returning to the room where she serviced her clients, he took her back to the house in Vitrolles which Carswell had reconnoitred before the mission began.

LeKahn kept her there all night, and although he gave her treble her usual fee when she left, the Corsican had beaten her up savagely on her return. It was the first time she'd spent the night out and he was convinced she'd cheated him of her earnings. She was badly enough hurt to have to go to hospital. When the Corsican collected her on her discharge, she ran away from him in the street.

For three days she'd roamed the northern quarter of the city, sleeping out on benches and terrified to go near the docks in case the Corsican found her again. Finally, exhausted and starving, having been attacked and refused payment by a trucker she'd hustled in the Parc Corderie, she made her way back to Vitrolles and after a day's hunting found LeKahn's house again.

He was out when she got there and she spent the evening hidden inside the canvas frame shed where he kept his dustbins. On his return at midnight, LeKahn took her inside, told her to strip in the tiny lounge and lay down on her there on the floor. Afterwards he got up, dressed again and told her what she had to do. She was to clean the house, cook his meals and wash his clothes; that was all—that and being available whenever he wanted her. He never asked why she'd returned. He merely put on his jacket, tied his tie and went out again.

A week later the Corsican traced her to the house. She managed to keep him out until LeKahn got back. The fight which followed lasted less than a minute. An hour afterwards an ambulance appeared and took the Corsican away; he'd been lying unconscious on the pavement in the meantime, his face kicked in and both his knee-caps smashed. LeKahn had never even mentioned the incident.

That had been a year and a half ago. She'd lived with the Belgian ever since.

'This was the first time I've been away. I mean, not just for a holiday but almost the first time out of Vitrolles since I went with Jean. We had a drive along the coast one Sunday when Jean had to see someone, that was all—'

Her head tilted forward again as the air began to grow warmer with the rising sun.

'Oh *merde!*' She heaved herself back on the seat. 'Can't I just sleep—just for a little? In a moment I won't even remember my name.'

'You'll be able to sleep soon, Minette—'

Carswell was already searching for a place to turn off the road.

'I'll find somewhere to stop. Then we'll have another try and see if we really can't get to it this time. Afterwards, you can sleep forever as far as I'm concerned.'

He saw the track a few minutes later.

It ran south from the road deep into the forest before curving out of sight to the left. Carswell glanced in the mirror; there was no sign of anyone ahead or behind. He swung the wheel sharply and set off through the trees.

Twenty minutes later they came to an open glade with a stream running along one side. The grass at the centre was bright green and studded with yellow flowers. Carswell stopped the car, got out and walked round to the passenger side.

'Come on, you can wash. That should freshen you up.'

He helped her out and, with his arm round her waist, half carried her over to a bank above the stream. She dropped to her knees, lowered her head towards the water and began splashing it over her face. Carswell walked further up the bank to a wide rocky pool, took off his clothes and plunged in.

The water was clear and icily cold and he gasped as it flowed over him. He stayed there, floating in the shallows, until he was almost numb. The sun was high and hot overhead and the air hummed with insects. He got out, dried himself with handfuls of bracken, dressed again and looked back at Minette.

She was still kneeling on the bank. She'd washed off the last of the make-up and she must have dipped her hair in the stream; it was scraped back behind her ears, shining wet and black on her neck, and for the first time he could see her face, still reddened in patches where he'd hit her but otherwise clean and pale. As he watched she threw back her head towards the sun, closed her eyes and knelt there motionless with the tips of her fingers trailing in the water.

Carswell walked back and stopped beside her. She must have been too exhausted to hear him because she didn't notice when he bent down and scooped up a handful of water. He reached out, pulled the neck of her blouse forward and poured the water inside.

She jumped to her feet and screamed.

'Bastard!'

She pulled the blouse out of her jeans and held it away from her body. Then, with what seemed to be her reflex response, she lashed out at him with her leg.

Carswell skipped back and laughed.

'Come on, we're going to try again—'

He turned, spotted a large pine tree on the far side of the clearing and started towards it.

'We'll sit under there in the shade. I'll get the map from the car and you can join me as soon as you're dry.'

'You little prick!'

She watched him walk away, holding her blouse out in front of her. For once there'd been comparatively little malice in her voice.

It was at midday, exactly four hours later, that Carswell finally proved himself right.

The morning was blazingly hot and Minette's shirt was sodden again, partly with sweat and partly with the water that Carswell collected every half hour from the stream in one of the Evian bottles and poured over her. 'Like watering a valuable plant,' he'd said once, but she hadn't smiled. Lying with her back propped against the trunk, her eyes glazed and her face puffy with fatigue, she looked incapable of any response apart from her slurred replies to his questions.

He was taking her through the events of Wednesday. Wednesday was the day on which LeKahn had driven through the village where Carswell had been expecting him to stop for the night. The Belgian might have made his discovery at any time the previous day, but he'd left that morning in the leisurely style of the entire week and when Carswell saw him again at five everything had changed.

It was during those few hours that LeKahn must have found out and told the girl. Carswell's conviction of that was becoming an obsession, and he returned to the day again and again.

'After coffee he had his anis—'

'Can you remember what brand it was, Minette? The shape of the bottle? The label?'

He was making her concentrate on details this time, forcing her to remember colours, shapes, smells, textures; hoping desperately that the answer would emerge from the mosaic of trivia.

'It was a square bottle, he had the same every day, sort of like this—'

Her hand traced a lazy shape in the air while her forehead puckered in concentration.

'The bottle was red and yellow with a horse on it.' She nodded. 'A small black horse. I remember now, I was looking at it one morning—'

She broke off. Carswell waited. Then he reached out his

hand and shook her lightly in case she'd drifted off to sleep.

'Go on, Minette, what else?'

'What's that?'

She hadn't been asleep. Her eyes were open and she was pointing over his shoulder. Carswell was sitting facing her, with his back to the brilliant sunlit space of grass outside the tree-shadow. He turned and looked behind him.

For a moment there was nothing; just the flat expanse of the turf with the wall of trees on the far side. Then something drifted quickly across the grass, a dark sickle-shaped shadow that raced over the clearing and vanished above them.

A few seconds later it came back, fast and silent, sweeping the glade like a razor-edged pendulum. He shifted his head and peered up through the laced branches of the tree. He couldn't see what he was looking for but he knew it was there: a hawk, a spade-tailed kestrel hunting the forest along the warm currents of midday air funnelled up by the valleys and ridges.

He turned back to Minette. 'That's a hawk's shadow. It's up there somewhere, hunting for mice or rabbits, I'd guess. Why?'

She didn't say anything, but she leant forward gazing at the grass. Carswell waited.

Then he said, 'All right, let's get back to the anis—'

'That's what I saw.' She didn't seem to have heard him. 'It was exactly the same. I saw it when we stopped.'

Carswell looked at her intently.

'When did you stop, Minette?'

'The day we were talking about, Wednesday.'

'Whereabouts?'

'I'm trying to think.' She hesitated. 'Yes, it was at a junction so Jean could look at the map.'

'Was it the morning or after lunch?'

'The afternoon. We'd been driving and it was all sort of bare and sandy and we stopped—'

Carswell nodded. The route was still vivid in his mind and

he knew to within twenty or thirty miles where it must have been; an intersection on the plain south of Tarragona. They'd have crossed it an hour or so after he'd made his daily check on their progress.

'There was this field, well, not a field really, more just earth and scrub, all dry and yellow.' She was still watching the glade. 'Jean had the map and I saw it, just the same, there—!'

She pointed as the shadow swung over the grass again, hovered for an instant at the centre of the clearing, then floated away.

'That's it! And I said, "Look, what's that?" And Jean looked up and said the same as you: "It's a hawk hunting." We could see it, very high and sort of still—'

She stopped again.

'What happened then?'

'I can't remember, really. I only remembered because of seeing it again now. Except it was funny in a way. Jean wasn't interested in anything like that, but he sat looking at it for hours, well, a few minutes, anyway. Then he laughed and we went on.'

'Didn't he say anything?'

'I don't think so. We just drove on.' She paused. 'Yes, he did say something like "We'll be going faster now." But that was only because we'd been hanging about all the time, and it was getting hotter and hotter and I was hating it.'

'Minette, think—'

Carswell was sitting up straight now. He took her wrist and shook it urgently.

He didn't know how or why yet, let alone what it was that LeKahn had discovered, but he was suddenly sure that it had happened then. They'd been driving along as before, LeKahn had stopped to consult his map, Minette had seen a hawk's shadow, the Belgian had watched the bird for several minutes, then he'd laughed and set off again—saying that in future they'd be travelling faster.

Something was still missing, some link to explain the whole sequence which had started with the hawk and ended with LeKahn driving beyond the night's stopping-place.

'That can't have been all Jean said. There must have been something more, something about the map, maybe? I don't know—*something!*'

She sat looking at the glade with her forehead wrinkled. Then she shook her head.

'No, nothing else. I asked him and he told me what it was and—'

Suddenly she swung round to face him.

'I know: Jean said it was a hawk, then a bit later he said its name. It was afterwards that he laughed.' She shrugged. 'Anyway, I thought it was the bird's name. Only, it was funny, because it belonged to a girl.'

'A girl? Hawks have names like—'

Carswell tried to remember the French patois names for the hawks LeKahn might have recognized. He repeated as many as he could, but she looked at him blankly.

'No, nothing like that,' she said. 'I'm sure it was a girl's name, very ordinary. Christ, I don't know, maybe it was just a joke—'

'Try to remember, Minette, try!'

Carswell clenched her wrist and pushed himself closer, willing her to think back to the hot dusty afternoon forty-eight hours earlier when that brief bizarre exchange with LeKahn had taken place.

For a few moments she was silent. Then she smiled, the first time she'd done so, and yawned again.

'That was it,' she said. 'I know why I thought it was so funny; a fucking girl's name for a bird like that. It made me laugh.'

'What was it, Minette?'

'Anna. You know, like the butter Tante Anna, and things like that—'

She went on smiling.

Carswell let go of her wrist. He dug his hands in the bed of leaves and squeezed the pine-needles against his palms until they pricked his skin, trying to clear the haze of weariness from his mind.

'Anna?' he repeated. 'Are you sure, Minette?'

'Honest, promise you.'

'Anna—'

Carswell relaxed his hands, let the pine-needles trickle out between his fingers and swivelled to look at the glade again. The shadow was still scything backwards and forwards over the grass.

He stood up, closed his eyes and leant against the tree-trunk. Below him the girl had already fallen asleep. She could sleep for as long as she wanted now. In a moment he'd sleep himself.

He'd been right. LeKahn had discovered where Samir was hidden and he had communicated the knowledge to the girl. London's gamble had paid off. They'd chosen a man who knew Samir, knew him because the Belgian was half-Arab himself, knew his habits, his fears, his needs, the patterns and workings of his mind. Rich and privileged, raised in a feudal society, loving sunlight, space, air, at home in the terrain of his own country where he could practise, as he'd done since a child, the ritual desert sports he'd followed passionately all his life.

It had needed only the image of a hawk's shadow in the sand for LeKahn to realize where in all Spain Samir would choose to live as an exile.

A million acres of sand and plain and marsh, salt flats and dry grass, horses, birds and fighting bulls, the largest and most desolate wild-life sanctuary in Europe—half the length of the country from that glade in the Guadalajara mountains.

Anna. The Coto of Doñana.

10

Teruel

Carswell was even more exhausted than he'd thought.

He'd intended to sleep for three or four hours, but when he woke again the light was already draining from the sky. It was eight; he'd been asleep since midday. He walked over to the stream, stripped naked again and slipped back into the water. Then he lay for a while on the rocks that bordered the pool, still warm with the stored heat of the day's sun. Afterwards he dressed, lit a fire near the pine tree and brewed some coffee. Minette never stirred as the flames crackled upwards.

The Coto Doñana. A guess, yes, it was still only that. But it had satisfied LeKahn and it satisfied Carswell—satisfied him enough to accept it as the one crucial piece of information he needed to take over the Belgian's role and continue the mission. London had obviously programmed for both the Americans' intervention and the expenditure of LeKahn if his trail was picked up. That was why they hadn't assigned him just a follower, but a follower who'd been instructed to operate under the war rules.

Carswell glanced at the date-window of his watch. It was May 14. The brief had stated that the serial must be finished by May 27. It left him with thirteen days.

There was one inflexible law that applied to all field operations regardless of how they'd been mounted: if a mission was threatened with exposure or neutralization, the field agent severed all contact with his control and continued alone. Known as the cut-out point, it was a legacy of wartime action in enemy territory when communications had been the most vulnerable element in any mission.

Carswell sipped his coffee. In the Robespierre serial, he decided, the cut-out point had come with LeKahn's death. London would realize quickly enough what had happened: they'd learn LeKahn had been killed, they'd know Carswell, his follower, had got away, and when he didn't make contact, they'd assume he was continuing with the mission as planned.

From now until the Robespierre serial was completed he'd maintain total silence.

The hunt for the killers of the Belgian and the posada manager was the next problem. It would already be under way. The police would probably have found the Ford, they'd have a full description of the girl, a partial one of himself and, if his guess about the Americans' luck was correct, almost nothing on them. All he could hope was that the Simca had escaped any connection with the two murders: the Coto was five hundred miles away and there was most of Spain to cross before he got there.

Finally, there was the girl. He glanced towards the pine tree and saw that Minette had just woken. She sat up, blinking sleepily, then she crawled under the branches and came over to the fire.

'Christ, that's better—'

She stretched her arms and yawned. By then the light had gone and the glade was full of pale-grey dusk.

'Coffee?' She sniffed at Carswell's mug. 'Is there any left?'

'I'll make some more.'

While he heated the water, she went to the stream and washed. Then she sat down beside him.

'Christ, that's good—'

She drank silently, rinsing the coffee round her mouth and smiling with pleasure.

'Gets you right in the belly, doesn't it? Next thing's a bite to eat. Hey—'

She broke off and looked at him, suddenly remembering the morning.

'Was that right, you know, that name Jean told me? I must have fallen asleep soon as I said it.'

'You did.' Carswell nodded. 'But, yes, it was right.'

'And was it what you wanted?'

'Yes.'

'That's good.' She sipped the coffee again. 'Now we can start getting back to France. If we wait a bit longer and then drive, really drive, we can probably get to the border before it's light again. Then—'

She'd obviously thought about nothing else since she'd woken and she had everything worked out; she even knew of a man in Marseilles who'd forge a French entry stamp on their passports.

'Costs a bit,' she said as she finished, 'but the way he does it, it's fucking marvellous; I mean you wouldn't know it wasn't stamped by the pigs themselves.'

'Minette, listen—'

Carswell looked at her and shook his head. He'd been about to consider the problem when Minette woke. Now, gazing at her across the flames, he realized that however long he'd thought about it, he wouldn't have found the answer.

He'd promised to get her back to France, to put her on a train or something. That might have been just possible if he'd learned LeKahn's destination within an hour of leaving the village; he'd have had the whole night before the police hunt started. But now, twenty-four hours later, it was inconceivable to think of heading north—the opposite direction from that Carswell had to go and immediately into the area where the search would be concentrated.

Yet what were the alternatives? To abandon her there in

the glade? She'd be picked up within thirty minutes of reaching the road; she'd inevitably tell the police everything that had happened, including the information about the Coto Doñana—whose significance they'd understand even if she still didn't; and any possibility of completing the mission would be ended within an hour.

Or to take her with him? A nineteen-year-old city girl without a word of Spanish, her description in the hands of every policeman in Spain and five hundred miles of country to cross before they even reached the Coto—that was even more inconceivable than to leave her behind.

Carswell shut his eyes for a moment, cleared his mind with a deliberate concentrated act of will and began to get to his feet.

There was no other option. Korea; Lisbon a decade earlier, when a former SS major had reached for his gun as Carswell looked down and he'd hit the man without even lifting his head; the posada manager at the foot of the stairs last night. Each time an immediate unthinking reflex response.

Unthinking—because that was the only tolerable way to act and then live with what you did. To chill oneself, dry oneself, to scour and cauterize every last nerve-end of feeling and emotion. Yes, there'd always be circumstances to explain and justify what happened. Finally, they were all irrelevant. The actions you took were determined in advance by the nature of the world you'd chosen to live in. Carswell had lived in the world of espionage and counterintelligence for almost thirty years—his entire adult life.

He didn't even need to analyze what the situation required of him now. He tossed his cigarette into the fire, put his hands on the ground and started to rise.

'No—'

Minette had stood up and was watching him across the fire, the mug clenched in her hand. Her voice was quiet and her eyes were looking steadily into his, wide-open and unblinking.

'All right, you can try and you'll do it, sure you'll do it. You're bigger and it's your filthy fucking business, isn't it? Just like Jean. But don't think you'll do it easy; Christ, you won't—'

She shook her head.

'I'll fight you long as I can. I don't care it won't make any fucking difference. Maybe I'll get lucky first, just for a moment, that's all, just to give you something you'll remember.'

'Minette—'

'Don't fucking Minette me! You ponce, you dirty lying little ponce—!'

Her face stiffened with anger.

'I trusted you the first time; I was so fucking scared I didn't know Christmas from my crutch. Then I did it again because I was too bloody tired to keep my eyes open. Twice! Poor pathetic stupid little bitch, aren't I? Well, not any more, I'm not. You've got what you want, I'm just something you're lumbered with. So fuck the promises, let's give her a chop on the neck like she was some sick rabbit and tidy her away. Fine, just come and try!'

'You're wrong—'

'Oh, I am, am I? Well, now, why don't you explain then?'

She lowered the mug and once again Carswell was taken in. As he frowned, trying to think what to say, she hurled the coffee into his eyes.

He was still squatting and the shock of the scalding liquid threw him back on his heels. He lurched sideways and tumbled to the ground. A moment later something glanced off his head and thudded into the earth beside him. Blinded and dizzy he wriggled away from the heat of the fire and rubbed frenziedly at his face.

Then a silhouette appeared above him, dark and blurred against the greyness of the sky, and something glittered like a coronet of diamonds in the air. The glitter plunged down towards his face; he jack-knifed sideways, scrambled to his feet and raced stumbling in the direction of the stream, guided by the splashing of the water.

By the time he reached the bank he could see again. The girl was a few yards behind holding a broken jagged bottle by the neck. Carswell waited, his hands in front of his face as if he was still blinded. She gathered herself and leapt forward, slashing at his neck. He swung back, the bottle glanced off his shoulder, then he tensed his leg and kicked high at her arm. He was wearing the hard-capped leather boots he'd worn all week, and the point of his toe caught the underside of her elbow.

She dropped the bottle, screamed, folded onto the grass and knelt there vomiting. Carswell kicked the bottle into the water and knelt down, his hand stiffening into a wedge of bone.

As he did so she opened her eyes and blinked, looking up at him with a steadfast bitter gaze.

'Well, don't hang about, you little prick—'

She was shuddering with pain, her face was grey and the word came out in a half-whisper.

'Because that's it then, isn't it? Fifty francs when it's over and the service isn't *compris, monsieur. Salaud!*'

She sucked at her mouth and tried to spit. The saliva gathered on her lips but wouldn't come out. Instead it trickled down her chin.

Carswell didn't move for a moment. Then he stood up, walked back to the stream and picked up the half-shattered bottle from where it was lying on the pebbles. He pressed his thumb against its neck and began to fill it with water.

It wasn't the bitter uncompromising defiance to the last, or the returning image of a worn St. Christopher medallion that had momentarily seemed to hover on the collar of her vomit-stained blouse. It was something else. Fifty francs. He knew that price. Unrecognized and unacknowledged he'd paid it all his life. The price of a way to endure and survive. His way—and Minette's.

He went back to the girl and began pouring the water slowly over her face, wiping it away with his sleeve when it began to run down into her eyes.

11

Cuenca

'Where are we going?'

Carswell peered at the map in the dashboard light.

'We'll try to get to a town called Cuenca,' he said. 'That's about two hundred miles south-west from here. It's on the main railway line and we can get a train—'

It was the best he'd been able to work out. The two hundred miles would be over the same bad mountain roads they'd driven along since leaving the coast, but they should be able to make the town before daylight. Once there it was a day's journey south by rail to Sevilla. Then they'd have less than a hundred miles in front of them to the Coto.

Everything depended, of course, on his guess that the police wouldn't be looking for the Simca. He'd only learn that when they were back on the road. Carswell looked up from the map at the girl.

She was sitting beside him in the passenger seat, staring ahead into the trees and holding her elbow with her hand. It was half an hour since he'd kicked her, but he'd caught the sciatic nerve and the pain would still be considerable. They'd barely spoken since.

'How are you feeling?'

He waited a moment. She didn't answer, so he added, 'Have you ever used a map?'

'Show me where you want to go.'

She bit out the words without looking at him. Carswell leant across and traced the route in pencil. For the first few hours it was going to be difficult; they'd be using the maze of forest tracks and if they took a wrong turning it could take them miles out of their way.

'I can do it.'

She snatched the map and spread it out on her knee. Then she glanced at him.

'Well, what the hell are you waiting for?'

Carswell turned the car in the glade and set off along the rutted path towards the road.

The first hour was much like the night before. It was dark by then, the road rose and fell through a succession of valleys and an occasional truck passed in the opposite direction. There were no cars and no sign of any *guardia civil*. After they'd driven for thirty miles Carswell decided they were probably safe. Then he saw the road-block. He turned a corner and a light shone in front of them. For a moment he thought it was the window of a woodman's cottage. Then as they came closer he noticed a parked van and a red-and-white-striped pole. There was a second light beyond the first and the silhouette of a caped figure crossed before it.

He braked and looked quickly at Minette. She'd also seen the lights and was gazing forward into the darkness.

'Get down on the floor,' he said. 'And hold tight. Don't look up whatever happens.'

Carswell switched off the ignition and the engine coughed. He waited, switched it on again, gunned the accelerator so that they picked up speed, then turned it off once more. There were further coughs and the car coasted gently onto the verge. The block was about twenty yards away.

He opened the door and got out, kneeling down in the pool of light from the headlamps and peering under the chassis.

'*Que pasa?*'

The shout came from the darkness ahead.

'I don't know,' Carswell called back in Spanish. 'Maybe it's the plugs.'

He slid back into the seat, keeping the door open, and pretended to reach for the bonnet catch. There were two men, the leading one less than ten yards away now, the other just behind. Their booted feet rang on the roadway as they approached.

'Let's have a look—'

The man's voice was close to the bonnet. As the outline of his head and shoulders appeared in the windscreen, Carswell snapped off the lights, started the engine, slammed his foot down on the accelerator and dragged the door shut.

As the car surged forward the leading man shouted and jumped sideways. An instant later the second one dived for the verge. Then the car smashed through the wooden pole, swerved round another corner and came out onto a deserted stretch of forest road.

'All right, you can sit up now.'

Minette got up from where she'd been lying hunched on the floor.

'The *flics?*'

'A road-check. Just two of them, *guardia civil.*'

'Won't they follow us?'

Carswell shook his head. 'All they've got is a scooter and a van. They could probably catch a sleepy mule but not much else.'

'What'll they do then?'

'They—'

He saw it as he started to answer, three lighted windows in a low white hut ahead of them. Carswell braked, drove slowly past, then accelerated again when they'd rounded the next corner.

'They'll get back there.' He jerked his head over his shoulder. 'It's a *guardia civil* post. There'll be others inside it, a telephone, everything they need.'

'And a car?'

'No, but they won't need one. They'll telephone forward. Within twenty minutes there won't be a *guardia* in the whole mountains who isn't looking for us.'

As he spoke Carswell pulled to the side and took the map from her.

A few miles ahead the road forked: the route he'd intended to take lay up the left arm. Now they'd have to abandon the car altogether. There'd be *guardia civil* posts every twenty or thirty miles whatever route they chose. The only alternative was to take to the hills and walk.

Just before the junction a small track ran off to the left. It climbed circuitously into the mountains and then, according to the map, petered out into nothing. It was probably a logging trail like the one which led down to the glade. Although they'd only be able to drive a few miles along it, the track had the advantage of running due south away from the coast and the French border—the direction the police would assume they'd taken.

Carswell put away the map and glanced down at the girl's light sandals.

'How do you like walking?' he asked.

'I hate it.'

'Well, you can start flexing your ankle muscles. There's a lot coming your way.'

It took them five minutes to reach the point where the track started.

Half an hour later he had to stop. By then they'd climbed to five thousand feet. Carswell got out and looked round. They'd reached a small clearing in the woods with a half-ruined thatched hut on one side and a great pile of small dry branches on the other—lopped off the felled trunks and discarded as worthless for timber. The track ended at a sandy bank. Beyond, a foot-path wound further up into the trees.

'This is where we start, Minette.'

She opened her door and stood watching him as he made a quick inventory of their possessions.

The girl had nothing apart from the clothes she was wearing, the sweater he'd made her bring and her make-up case. He took the case, emptied the litter of bottles and jars onto the front seat, and handed it back to her. She shrugged but said nothing. Then he went through his own suitcase, took out a few clothes and packed them into a canvas bag.

Afterwards, he went over to the hut. It had probably been used for stabling the oxen that dragged the logging carts down to the road. He cleared the fallen thatch from the doorway, drove the Simca inside and rearranged the straw so that the car was completely hidden. Finally, he roped LeKahn's gun-case to the canvas bag, swung the pack onto his shoulders and looked at Minette.

'Ready?'

She nodded. 'How far?'

It was another chill night. As far as Carswell could tell the clearing was midway up a ridge whose peak he could just see against the skyline ahead. Somewhere about two hundred miles beyond was Cuenca. He smiled in the darkness.

'About five or six days,' he said. 'That's if we're lucky and can keep going straight. If we're not, if we have to make detours, then it could take us twice as long.'

'Ponce!'

He turned, chuckling, and she followed him towards the path.

They walked for eight hours that first night.

The sky was as clear as the night before. Cuenca was almost due south of the clearing where they'd left the car. For the first few miles the path followed the ridge upwards in the right direction. Then it swung away to the west and he had to cast round in the trees before he found another that continued south. Afterwards there was a succession of paths, all winding along the hill crests. The ground underfoot was firm and sandy and although there were deep rifts on either side, the paths kept to the same altitude and the going was easy.

The air grew colder as the night wore on, but the thick sweaters kept them both warm. Carswell took a break every two hours, measuring the time exactly and never stopping for more than ten minutes. Occasionally he'd turn to ask Minette if she was all right. She'd nod or grunt a brief affirmative but that was all. Once he offered to carry her empty make-up case but she merely shook her head and walked on. She was obviously stronger than she looked; there was something wiry and hard-wrought, the sinewy toughness of a street child, in her tall thin frame. Glancing at her feet, Carswell wondered how she'd be by the end of the second day.

When they took the third break, she put her bag down and asked him for a cigarette.

Carswell gave her one and said, 'You haven't smoked before.'

'I do sometimes.' She drew on the cigarette, holding it slanted down between her thumb and forefinger. 'What are these?'

'*Ducados,* black tobacco. If you like something milder, I'll get you what the Spanish call *rubios* when I can find somewhere to buy them.'

'What's that?'

'It means blond, really, but they use it for light tobacco like American cigarettes.'

She shook her head. 'These are okay.'

Carswell watched her. Even in the darkness her hair was very black. Half closing his eyes he realized it was what anyone would notice and remember first; the dark thick tangle surrounding her pale face. He didn't say anything then, but he decided he'd have to do something about it as soon as he could.

When they stopped for the fourth time it was almost dawn; in less than an hour there'd be full daylight. Carswell left her in a copse where he'd put down the baggage and walked along the path.

Mist covered the landscape but he could see the outline of a valley below him to the west with a river at its centre. At one point there seemed to be a ford; the light glinted on an expanse of shallow water and the sand on either side was pitted with wheel tracks. Beyond it a cluster of small white buildings was huddled against the trees. Smoke was rising from the chimneys and a couple of dogs were yelping on the shore. There was no sign of a road.

He went back to the copse. Minette was slumped under a tree.

He said, 'Are you tired?'

'What the hell do you think?'

'You've been doing fine. I reckon we've covered close to thirty miles.'

She shrugged and began to take off her shoes.

'How are your feet? Can I take a look?'

'Leave my fucking feet alone!'

The words blazed out as Carswell leant forward. He hesitated a moment. Then he turned away, walked to the other side of the copse and settled himself down under the trees.

'We'll sleep for about six hours,' he said. 'If I'm gone when you wake, don't worry. There are some houses down in the valley and I'm going to try to buy some food. Keep out of sight until I get back.'

There was no reply. He waited for ten minutes. Then he raised himself on one elbow and looked across at her. She was lying sprawled on her back breathing steadily, with her eyes closed. Her shoes were a few feet away beside the make-up case.

Carswell crawled over, picked up the sandals and tucked

them under his sweater. There was nowhere she could go, nothing she could do without him, but he wasn't prepared to take any chances. A few moments later he fell asleep.

Carswell was woken by his shoulder being shaken violently. He opened his eyes and saw the girl kneeling beside him. It must have been soon after he'd gone to sleep because the sky was still grey and there were stars above the tree-tops.

'Where are my shoes?'

'They're here—'

'I want them,' she snapped.

He lifted himself on his elbow. 'Why?'

'Because my feet are fucking cold and I want to put them on. That's why!'

Carswell pulled her shoes out and gave them to her.

'What did you think I was going to do? Run away?'

'You've been stupid before, Minette—'

'*Cochon!*'

She gazed down at him, her body rigid with anger and resentment.

'You've lied to me all the way down the line. I've taken it all, too, just like I'm taking it now. Because I'm stuck with you, because I haven't got any fucking option. I hate it, and I hate you, only I'm not a fool. Understand? You get your dirty little mind round that and stop treating me like one!'

'All right, I'm sorry.'

She spat, walked back to where she'd been lying and soon afterwards they were both asleep again.

Minette was still asleep when he woke. The sun was high and the heat had brought out the resinous scent of the pine-needles. Carswell glanced at his watch: it was eleven o'clock. He rinsed his face in a handful of water from the remaining Evian bottle. Then he set off down the hillside towards the settlement—bright now in the sunlight.

He reached the ford, rolled up his trousers and waded across; the water was cold, mountain water carried down from the peaks to the north, and trout were rising to feed at the river's centre. On the far bank he dried his feet in the sand, put on his boots and walked into the little village.

There were five or six houses with clay-pot roofs and a bar that doubled as a shop. Carswell went inside, blinking at the darkness after the sun, and sat down at a table. For a few minutes the place was deserted. Then an old man of about seventy, dressed in striped trousers with brass-buckled braces over a dirty grey shirt, appeared through a door that led to the back.

'*Buenas.*' He swabbed down the table.

Carswell returned the greeting. 'You got any cold beer?'

The old man grunted and jerked his thumb towards an ancient icebox in the shadow at the back of the room.

'Come far?'

'Far enough.' Carswell shrugged. 'Madrid. Got a cousin in Barcelona, doing well with a couple of trucks and wants me to drive one for him.'

The old man nodded. 'How come you're heading this way for Barcelona?'

'Got a ride to Priego yesterday, but there wasn't anything on the road after that. I thought I'd cut through the hills and try again at Monreal—'

Carswell had worked out the story before he left the copse. He yawned and stretched his legs.

'It's further than I thought,' he added.

'It's a walk.'

'Still, I should make Monreal tonight. Then a truck tomorrow and I'll be there by lunch.'

'Maybe.'

The old man went back to the bar. Carswell emptied half the bottle and swung round towards him.

'Get many people passing through?'

'Here?' The old man snorted derisively. 'Who wants to come here? Bunch of loggers in winter, the *señoritos* in summer—

if they're fishing up-river and want a drink. That's all. Not counting the Chinamen, that is.'

'Chinamen?'

'That's what I said.' The old man laughed. 'They invading us or something? Came from the *guardias,* it did. Had a patrol through here this morning, well, just before you. Said they've got the whole force out looking for them, two men and a girl, with one of them Chinese. Stole a car and ran it through a block up Monreal way last night—'

The old man laughed again as he washed up some glasses in a sink behind the bar.

'You ask me, most of those *guardias* wouldn't know a Chinaman from their arse!'

Carswell finished his beer. In one way they'd obviously been lucky. He must have been wrong in thinking no one had seen the Filipino in the village where LeKahn was killed; someone had noticed him and the man's description was the logical one for the police to fasten onto. It was inevitable they'd be looking for Minette too, although there'd be no way of discovering whether Carswell was the third person they were after.

The rest of what he'd learned was less welcome. Carswell had been virtually certain that the hunt would be directed towards the north. But if a patrol had been sent south to a hamlet as small as this, it meant they were either searching in every direction or concentrating on the Teruel-Guadalajara mountains. That in turn suggested that they'd found the Simca.

The implication of the car's hiding-place would be unmistakeable. Anyone heading for the French border would have abandoned it where the hills dropped to the Tarragona plain—the plain LeKahn had been crossing when he'd seen the shadow of the hunting hawk. The logging stable where Carswell had left it was in the opposite direction; from there the clear inference would be that the occupants had taken to the mountains and were moving south on foot.

Whatever the explanation for the *guardias'* visit, it was obvious that the sooner he and the girl moved on the better.

Carswell stood up and walked over to the counter. There were boxes of fruit and vegetables at one end, and the shelves behind were laden with groceries.

'If I'm not going to make Monreal until dark, I'd better have something to eat on the way,' he said.

He bought some bread, lentils, fruit, olive oil and then, as the old man turned to lift down a length of dried sausage, Carswell noticed a cardboard tray full of hair bleach sachets. He slipped two of them into his pocket before the man turned back, paid his bill and went to the door.

'Up the river,' he said, 'then across at the next ford and after that straight north?'

The old man nodded. 'There's a track on the other side. If you don't make Monreal tonight, there are pueblos up there where you'll get a bed.'

'Thanks. And if I meet the Chinese army on the way?'

'Send a cable.' The old man laughed.

Minette was awake by the time he returned. She'd washed and she was sitting smoking as he came up through the trees. He could smell the smoke mingled with the scent of the pine-needles even before he saw her, but she didn't move until he stopped in the centre of the copse and put the package on the ground. Then she turned and stared at him expressionlessly.

'Hungry?' Carswell unpacked the food. 'I've got enough to last us until tomorrow. I've also learned a bit about what's going on behind us—'

'Doesn't make much difference, does it?' She said flatly, 'They'll get us sooner or later, just a matter of time.'

'Not if I can help it.' He glanced across. 'Can you cook?'

She inspected his purchases and shrugged.

'Real food, not that sort of stuff.' She prodded the *chorizo*. 'What's that, anyway? It stinks.'

'You'll see.'

Carswell went back into the wood, found a wind-fallen oak and broke off an armful of the smaller branches near its top. Then he began to strip them of the bark.

Squatting there, his knife whittling the wood into dry white chips, sun pattering the earth round him, the wind moving in the tall elms above, he might have been on any one of the trips he'd made into the hills over the years. Even before he'd been posted to Madrid he'd done the same from Brussels—days on end in the Ardennes or taking the train to Scharnhof in summer, walking until darkness in the Black Forest, sleeping in some village *Gasthaus,* moving on again at dawn.

Madrid was better than Brussels, yet it was still another city, another staging-post in which to carry out the same painstaking fragmented work—fragmented because one never saw the completed chain with each hard-won link strung together—another tidy empty apartment, another round of bars, another series of games of chess to fill the evenings.

The hills, everywhere, were different. Space and movement instead of the constricted hours of waiting in some parked car or subway telephone booth. Contact again with things that were solid, tangible, rounded: a river to be crossed, a fire to be made in the wind's lee, a meal to be cooked.

Perhaps, above all, they demanded and tested your self-sufficiency. In other places you survived and endured by paying a price to someone else: the price Minette paid, the price he paid himself. In the hills the only price asked was of yourself. Surviving there was more than just to endure: it was to win something back.

'What are you doing?'

Carswell looked up as Minette spoke.

'Peeling the bark from these?' He said, 'Because the wood burns faster and hotter without it, and then it's the bark which makes a fire smoke.'

He put a match to the pile of branches and fanned the fire

into a fierce smokeless blaze. Then he poured the lentils into a pan from his bag, sluiced in olive oil and water, and added the vegetables with some segments of the dried sausage. Finally, he snapped off a sprig of rosemary from a nearby bush, shredded the leaves over the surface and put the pan on the flames.

Thirty minutes later it was ready. Carswell ladled some out and tasted; the stew was hot and thick, flavoured with the strong smokey tang of the sausage and the lighter aromatic scent of the rosemary. He handed the ladle to Minette.

'Try it!'

She took a cautious mouthful, wrinkled her face, then sipped again. After a moment she nodded.

'What's it called?'

Carswell laughed. 'In Spanish it's a *cocido*—what the country people eat all over.'

She took another mouthful. 'What's the other smell? Not the *charcuterie,* the other one?'

'The rosemary? You're a French girl and you don't know rosemary? God Almighty, what do you usually eat?'

'Food.' She shrugged, swallowing hungrily now. 'What the hell do you think? Whatever they got in the supermarket. Jean didn't care: he liked tripe and beans, that was all. I do the special offers; you know, a free glass if you buy the big soap box. Those and the competitions—you can get really good things on them.'

Carswell laughed and broke another sprig off the bush.

'Here,' he said. 'It grows wild almost everywhere. It's meant to cure rheumatism and corns too; the country people dry it and burn it in their fires in winter. Smell!'

He crushed the sprig between his fingers and held it out to her. She took his hand and lifted it to her face, sniffing at the moist broken leaves.

When she looked up again Carswell realized it was the first occasion they'd had any physical contact which hadn't been part of a fight.

'How do you know all of that?'

She was watching him curiously. He took the ladle and began to eat.

'I just picked it up here and there, I suppose. Living alone, travelling, being out in the country often. Why?'

'Don't know.' She shook her head. 'Maybe you don't think of men knowing things like that, you know, cooking and that. You ever been married?'

Carswell didn't reply for a moment. Then he nodded.

'Well, maybe you learned from her?'

'I didn't learn anything from her, anything at all.'

He'd answered immediately, emphatically. As soon as he'd spoken, Carswell knew it wasn't true: he had learned a great deal from his wife; all of it had been bad.

'Why did you say *have* I been married?' He added, 'How do you know I'm not married now?'

'There's something about people married, sort of safe and easy.' Minette spat out a lump of gristle from the sausage. 'Like they know what they've got, where they are, even when it's bad. You can just tell. You haven't got it.'

She said nothing else until they'd finished eating and Carswell had made coffee. Then she took the mug, and as he was stamping out the fire, she looked at him again.

'You were really going to kill me yesterday, weren't you.'

It was a statement, not a question, coming abruptly out of the silence and the first time either of them had referred to the incident in the glade.

Carswell hesitated, his foot raised above a mound of glowing coals. Then he drove it into the ground.

'I suppose—'

'You don't "suppose" about killing people, you just do it. Yes or no.'

'All right then, yes, I was, Minette.'

'Well, why didn't you?'

He paused again. The fire was dead now and he was covering the ashes with leaves, scattering them over the charred circle of earth and brushing the ground smooth with bracken.

'Maybe because I thought you might be able to help me,' he said eventually. 'We've got a long way to go. You might—'

'*Merde!*' She cut him off. 'I'm just a fucking great nuisance. I can't even speak the language. You're like a cat with a tin can tied to its tail—'

She stopped and shook her head, frowning at him.

Then she added, 'You're a funny man.'

It was late dusk before they stopped again.

Carswell had intended to repeat the pattern of the previous night, taking a ten-minute break every two hours. But as he was about to halt for the first time, he noticed something dazzle briefly on a hill-flank to their right. He stopped, left Minette squatting in the undergrowth off the path they'd been following and crawled forward through the trees.

Immediately below him the ground fell steeply to the foot of a ravine. On the far side a line of *guardia civil* was combing through the brush. The most distant man was almost a mile away, high up on the crest, but the line ended in the ravine itself and the nearest was less than a hundred yards beneath Carswell. In all, there were about twenty of them, spaced evenly up the hill-flank; the flash of light had come from one of their cap badges.

As he watched, there was a shout, the line wheeled and began to sweep down the hill. The man below waited until the others came abreast of him. Then he started up the slope towards the trees where Carswell was kneeling.

Carswell turned and ran back to Minette. It would take the line only a few minutes to reach the path. There wasn't time for them either to run on ahead or to escape down the reverse side of the ridge. They'd certainly be seen if they tried the first, and the bushes on the far flank were so thick that they'd be heard forcing their way through long before they reached the bottom. All they could do was hide in the undergrowth and hope the men would miss them if the search crossed the path and continued down the other side.

He took her elbow and pulled her into the dense spiney maquis that covered the ground. A few yards from the path a pine tree, uprooted in some winter storm, lay tilted on its side. There was a low arch between the trunk and the earth with a network of ivy curtaining the space inside. Carswell parted the ivy and pushed her forward. Then he crept in beside her.

'Stay absolutely still and keep your face on the ground,' he whispered.

The line had almost reached the top of the ridge, and he could hear the men's voices.

Minette was lying pressed against him with her head flattened on the earth.

There was a shout as the first man found the path. He'd reached it directly opposite the fallen tree and his voice echoed through the bushes less than fifteen feet away.

A few minutes later the others joined him; more voices called out, there was the clatter of boots on rock, the sound of a match being struck and a burst of laughter.

Carswell waited, his head lowered under the screen of ivy. Then he dribbled some saliva into his palm, drew his hand over the rotting humus of leaves beneath the trunk, rubbed the mixture across his face, lifted himself up and looked out.

The men had gathered on the path and were taking a break; some of them had removed their caps and were sprawled on the sand, others were standing in groups, talking and smoking. All of them had been issued with rifles. The guns had been stacked in a neat wigwam with a bandolier draped across its top; the chequered sunlight, falling through the branches, gleamed on a line of bullets in the webbing sockets.

Five minutes passed. Then an officer appeared in the square of sun and shadow framed by the bushes. He gave an order, the men stood up, collected their rifles and arranged themselves in a casual column. A few moments later they vanished down the path in the direction from which Carswell and the girl had climbed up earlier.

Carswell gave them a further five minutes. Then, when he was sure they were out of earshot, he crawled under the arch and stood up stiffly.

'All right?'

Minette's voice was anxious. He glanced back as she eased her way out.

'For the moment.' Carswell nodded. 'But that's only because we got lucky. They're obviously searching every inch round here. Which means we get moving again—and this time we keep moving.'

The journey was much harder than the night before. Twice during the afternoon they saw other search parties. Each time they were further away than the first, but on both occasions it meant leaving the path and taking a wide detour down the hillside. The climbs back up to the ridges were difficult, long hard traverses of thorn and rock with the maquis pressing in on every side. Carswell himself had been panting when they regained the crests.

The second time he had to wait for several minutes before Minette caught up with him. When she reached the path again her face was white, her blouse was damp with sweat and the tendons were stretched tight against the skin of her neck. He was on the point of changing his mind and saying they'd take a rest, but she must have guessed what he was thinking. She shook her head stubbornly before he could speak, pushed past him and set off through the trees.

He finally stopped at eight. They'd been forced to leave the hog's-back ridges for a while and cut through a series of gulleys before finding another of the linked crests that led south. By then the air was grey with the oncoming darkness. They'd climbed halfway up the slope when Carswell saw a mountain spring bubbling out of the rocks in front of them.

'Time for an amateur cosmetics break—'

He swung the pack off his shoulders and put it down on a boulder beside the pool.

'What?'

Minette dropped to the ground.

'That jet-black bird's nest on top of your head,' he said. 'If we don't do something about it, it's going to give us away faster than anything else.'

There was a rocky defile near the mouth of the spring. Carswell made another fire, boiled some water and took the pan over to Minette. Then he tore a handkerchief into strips, poured one of the bottles of bleach into the water and set to work.

An hour later Minette had turned into a tawny blonde. The effect was somewhat streaky and there were patches near the roots where her hair had defied the peroxide, but over-all Carswell was satisfied. In the half-darkness it looked almost professional; certainly no one looking for a tall raven-haired girl would immediately connect her with Minette now.

'Take a look,' he said.

He handed her the make-up case in which he'd packed the rest of the food. She lifted the lid and peered at the mirror inside.

'*Mon dieu!*'

She gazed at herself for several moments, twisting her head from side to side.

'Like a bloody fading film-star, aren't I?'

Carswell laughed. 'It'll do for the moment. When we get to a town, we'll have it done properly—'

He turned, lifted the pack and swung it back over his shoulders.

'Come on.'

He climbed the defile, stopped and looked back.

Minette was still kneeling by the pool examining her reflection in the water. The surface shone like glass in the twilight and he could see the movements of her head, haloed by stars, as she tossed her hair. He waited a moment. Then he whistled; she heaved herself wearily to her feet and set off after him.

They climbed for a further five hours through the darkness. The ridges seemed endless. They'd reach the finish of one and for a while it would look as if the slope beyond at last fell down to a plain. But there would only be a saddle of rock, the ground would rise again and they'd come out onto another of the long hog's-back ribs running south. And always there'd be others when that one ended, other saddles and clefts and great banks of shale where the winter rains had washed the hillside bare, and they had to walk upwards half crouching, their feet scrabbling among the drifts of stone.

It was the third night without cloud, but now there was a light stinging wind. It rose soon after nine and blew steadily from behind their backs. In one way it was useful; at times Carswell could feel it help lift them up the hill-flanks. But it was Pyrenean wind, blowing straight from the snow-fields on the mountains to the north, and it cut viciously into the skin on their arms and necks, knifing its way under their clothes and chilling their bones.

At two Carswell decided they'd done enough. They'd walked for more than ten hours since they'd eaten; if they maintained the average speed he'd calculated for the previous night, they must have covered a further forty miles. It was about double what he'd guessed Minette would be capable of when they started. He turned to look at her.

'How are you feeling?'

'Like sleep—'

They were in another small clearing in the trees. She'd thrown herself down on the ground and was lying on her back, star-shaped in the darkness.

'Where are we?'

'Almost halfway.' He paused. 'How are your feet?'

'At the end of my legs when I last looked.'

'Can I see them?'

She didn't answer for a moment. Then she shrugged.

'Help yourself.'

She'd kicked off her shoes. Carswell could see the blood even before he touched her.

He squatted down, rolled her jeans up to her knees and examined each of her feet in turn; there were raw broken blisters on both soles, thorns had pierced the canvas caps of the sandals and lacerated her toes, and the skin on her heels had cracked open almost an inch up her swollen ankles.

'We'll eat first, then I'll see what I can do.'

There was a high bank on one side of the clearing. At one end of it the earth had fallen away, leaving a ribbon of the top-soil exposed. The soil was composed of the broken-down detritus of leaves and pine-needles, sun-dried into a shallow layer of peat.

Carswell pulled out his knife and dug strips from it, following the line of the fissure and taking only the lightest parts near the surface. He carried them over to where Minette was lying and stacked them in a pyramid over a heap of leaves beside her.

'What are you doing?'

She'd pushed herself up on one elbow and was watching him. Her face was drawn with tiredness in the bars of moonlight between the branches.

'Different sort of fire,' he explained. 'You use oak chips by day because they don't give off any smoke. At night smoke doesn't matter. What you can see is flame, this burns without it.'

Ten minutes later the peat was smouldering with a low red glow and a thin column of smoke was rising into the trees.

Carswell made another stew. When they'd eaten, he refilled the pan with water, dropped in a handful of juniper berries and let them boil for a while.

'Something else you just picked up here and there?'

The food had revived her and she leant forward sniffing at the pan.

Fatigue seemed to have drained her of hostility and her voice was quiet. It wasn't the tiredness of forty-eight hours ago, hard-edged and brittle from strain and lack of sleep. Instead it was the exhaustion of physical effort, the limp relaxation of having been pressed to the limit of her strength.

Carswell nodded, smiling. 'It's to cauterize the cuts, dry them out and keep them from going septic.'

'Will it hurt?'

'Yes.'

'Much?'

'The worst parts, yes.'

'Merde!'

He chuckled. 'Keep saying that and you'll feel it less.'

He washed off the blood and dirt. Then he lanced the weals and blisters that hadn't already broken.

She tensed when his knife cut into her skin and her wrists trembled as she clenched her hands. When he rubbed on the scalding mixture of water and juniper oil, her head jerked back and she cried out with pain. Afterwards, he could hear her muttering under her breath, a chain of curses that she repeated over and over again like a litany.

He worked the mixture into the cuts until the soles of both her feet were stained black. Then he poured some olive oil into his hand and slapped it against her heels, cupping the oil there until it had soaked into the skin.

'All right?'

He'd finished and was drying his palms on his trousers.

'Jesus fucking Christ, it stings!'

Carswell nodded. 'It will for a while, but at least they're clean and dry. When they've healed—and I'll have to keep doing it until they are—you'll be able to walk anywhere, any distance.'

'Anywhere I go after this, I go by cab.'

He laughed again. 'How about the legs?'

'They just ache.'

'We'd better deal with them too. Take your jeans off.'

She sat up, stared at him and opened her mouth. Then she shrugged and lay back. She unbuckled her belt and wriggled her jeans down to her ankles.

Carswell rolled her onto her stomach, knelt across her, slapped some oil onto her calves and thighs, and began to massage them. The muscles were knotted and hard, a series of small tight lumps under her skin, but fifteen minutes later they'd splayed out and felt supple beneath his fingers.

'Christ, that's better—'

She sat up, pulled her jeans back to her waist and yawned. Then she smiled quickly.

'Thanks.'

Carswell grinned back. 'Just don't go and break anything—that's more complicated.'

He kicked the smouldering segments of peat into a line a metre long.

'You've got four hours this time,' he said. 'Make the most of them. And lie with your back to the fire; it'll help stop the muscles stiffening again.'

He lay down on the other side. The smoke curled up through the branches, thick and sweet-scented.

A few minutes later they were both asleep.

They started again soon after three and walked until daylight.

Carswell lit another fire and cooked the last of the food. Then they set off once more. It was like that for the next three days. Twice Carswell went down into the valleys and replenished their supplies from a little store like the one he'd stopped at first; he learned nothing more about the police hunt and after the second day they saw no more search parties.

A shadowed path in the sunlight, a ten-minute break, cigarette smoke in the morning air, a climb through the afternoon heat, another break, a rocky track at dusk, a peat fire, further miles in the darkness with the wind at their backs and some stars cold, bright, patterning the mountain sky overhead before the moon came out. Hour after hour after hour until the whole journey became a continuum of movement, snatched chilling sleep, charcoal-tasting meals cooked in the shelter of some boulder-strewn gulley, interchange of sweat and frost, straining arms, shoulders, legs in movement again—the endless trudging along crests and ridges and spurs.

By midnight on the fifth night they'd travelled almost two hundred miles—forty miles in every twenty-four hours since they'd started. For Carswell alone and in the open it would have been achievement enough. Yet through the Teruel hill country, accompanied by the girl and under the constant tension of watching for the search, it was extraordinary. Twice that last day, plotting roughly where they were by peaks he identified on the map, Carswell found it difficult to believe quite how far they'd come.

Minette's feet were really bad by then. The oil he rubbed on her heels each time they stopped had prevented the cracks from widening, but the open sores grew worse. The juniper lye would dry the wounds for a while and none of them went septic, but after the first hour's walking they'd open again; the blood stained her sandals dark brown and in places the skin wore down to open flesh.

She never once complained, merely swearing rhythmically to herself as she followed him, but their progress grew slower and slower. They had to stop more often and whenever they did Carswell couldn't rest himself; he had to spend each break washing and massaging and bandaging. In a way he might have been treating something independent of her—they both felt that. He'd say her ankles looked better and Minette would nod approvingly, as if he'd congratulated her on buying a durable piece of equipment. Alternatively, when a new sore broke out she'd frown angrily while he was washing it, as if she'd been cheated by the factory.

Carswell had taken to carrying the make-up case which contained their food, and whenever they came to a steep slope he'd put his arm round her waist and pull her up. Before, she'd have shaken him off fiercely. Now she simply tolerated it, saying nothing, never even thanking him. They were both engaged in a common effort: to see if they could tote the luggage of her body to a point they'd jointly and tacitly agreed on.

Perhaps nothing else could have united them, Carswell thought once, except for the raw bruised lumps of her feet.

'About fifteen miles, I reckon, and we've made it—'

It was after twelve on the fifth night and they'd stopped for the evening's sleep. Once again they were in a clearing high up on a ridge and the wind was blowing strongly from the north.

'There seems to be another crest after this one,' he added. 'But that should be the last. Afterwards we drop down for few miles, and, God willing, we should find Cuenca and the train.'

Minette was too weary to answer for a moment. Her hair was tangled and matted, and in spite of exhaustion her face was no longer pale, but sun-tanned, with the skin flaking on her nose. Carswell had a fringe of beard and his eyes were bloodshot from constantly scanning the valleys below them.

She nodded, coughed and pointed at his pocket for a cigarette. Carswell lit one and gave it to her.

Then she asked, 'Aren't you going to make a fire?'

Carswell was already scooping out a trough in the pine-needles for her to lie in. He shook his head.

'Too risky, too many people around. There'll be hill farms from here onwards.'

He'd seen lights several times over the past two hours on the flanks beneath. It was unlikely that anyone would be out at that height in the darkness, but there was always the possibility that some shepherd might see the glow and climb up to investigate.

Minette shut her eyes, huddled herself in her sweater and shivered.

'You can come and sleep with me—'

Carswell stopped and rephrased it. 'I mean, come and lie here beside me. It'll help keep us both warm.'

She looked at him briefly. Then she rolled across the space that separated them and dropped into the trough, lying there rigid for a time with her back to him. Afterwards she relaxed. She was still smoking and Carswell could smell the acrid black tobacco as the wind whipped it past his face.

'What do we do when we get to that other town?'

Her voice coming out of the darkness was quiet but clear, as if she'd crossed a threshold of fatigue to a place where she barely needed sleep.

'You mean Sevilla—'

Carswell propped himself up on his elbow. Over the five days they'd hardly spoken except when he'd asked about her feet. LeKahn and the work he'd been doing hadn't been mentioned once.

'We'll find a place to stay. Then there's something I have to check. After that I'll finish what Jean was meant to do and then—'

'You didn't know Jean, did you?'

'No, I never even met him. The first time I saw him was across from his office in Marseilles just before you left. But we were still working together—'

'I knew Jean very well,' she cut him off again, and paused. 'Means I know you a bit too.'

'How's that?'

Carswell shifted himself to look at her. He could see her matted hair and the glowing tip of the cigarette, but her face was turned away.

'Means I think I know what you're going to do,' she said. 'Jean hurt people; Christ, it wasn't just his business, he *liked* doing it. If you've got to finish something for him, you don't exactly have to be a genius to guess what—not with that gun and all. Only—'

She broke off and drew on the cigarette. Carswell said nothing.

'Well, you're different, aren't you? You're not really like him. Know something? When you said it wasn't for money—and fucking hell, it would have been for Jean; he didn't pee unless someone paid him—well, when you said that, I believed you. Funny!'

There was silence for a moment. Then Carswell said, 'I do the same sort of work as Jean, Minette, so sometimes I have to be like him.'

'You didn't kill me; he'd have done if it'd been like that.'

'Maybe.'

'Fuck maybe! He'd have done it. Why not you?'

'I told you before—'

'You told me balls before, not the reason.'

Carswell dropped back onto the pine-needles. He felt hazy with exhaustion himself and his own legs were aching.

He didn't know the reason. He'd thought about what had happened many times over the five days and he still hadn't been able to find the answer. Once or twice he'd even regretted that he hadn't finished it when she was lying by the stream; everything since would have been so much easier. Now it was too late; there'd been a moment when it had been possible, the moment had passed, afterwards he was saddled with her—"a cat with a tin-can tied to its tail," as she'd described him.

The defiance, the intractable refusal to concede or plead when she knew it was all over, the recognition of himself in her—and the price they'd both opted to pay for the way they'd chosen to live. Yes, that was part of it. But part of it only. There'd been something else, something in Minette, something beyond payment, endurance, survival. Yet he still didn't know what it was. He'd been shaken by what he'd done as hadn't happened for years, for as long as he could remember.

Now, almost a week later, he was no closer to understanding why.

'I'm not sure, Minette,' he said. 'Just leave it.'

'But you killed that other man,' she went on stubbornly, 'the one in the pension. Now you're going to kill someone else. Only not me, you leave me out, and I'm in your way. Doesn't make sense, does it?'

'Shut up and go to sleep.'

Carswell settled himself firmly on his side and closed his eyes. Minette didn't say anything else and he went to sleep with the smoke from her cigarette still whirling past his face.

It was bitterly cold when he woke again. He lay on his back, blinking up at the branches. The rustle and curl of the leaves moved like surf. The cold must have built up while he'd slept and he could feel dampness in the wind that was still cutting icily overhead.

He woke Minette, turned her onto her stomach and spent five minutes chopping hard at her legs. Then he roped the pack onto his shoulders and they set off.

Cuenca came into sight at seven, a sprawl of grey buildings below them at the junction of two valleys, with the spider-line of the railway winding towards the south. Rain had been falling for an hour by then and they were both soaked; the water had sodden the ropes of the pack, and weals were starting to burn on his neck as the straps rubbed against the skin. Minette was stumbling and limping; in spite of the juniper lye a boil had formed on her ankle, and the swelling had reddened the leg up to her knee.

By the time they reached the town Carswell was almost carrying her. He avoided the main streets and worked his way round to the station. There was an express south in half an hour. They sat out the time in a damp shed, an abandoned mail-bag store. Minette slumped against him, her head on his shoulder and blood leaking from her sandals onto the floor. Then he bought two third-class single tickets and they boarded the train.

Ten hours later they were in Sevilla. It was eight o'clock. The light was golden on the yellow bricks of the old town and the streets were crowded with the evening *paseo*. Carswell found a small hotel near the station, checked in and they were shown up to a double-room on the second floor.

Minette was too exhausted even to undress. She fell onto the bed and slept immediately. Carswell managed to remove her jeans and her shirt, still moist with the dawn rain, and pushed her under the quilt cover. Then he struggled out of his own clothes and collapsed beside her.

He'd forgotten to draw the curtains and a violet neon clock above a jeweller's shop on the other side of the street shone through the window. Just before he fell asleep Carswell noticed the date in brilliant orange letters at its centre.

It was May 18. There were nine days left before the Robespierre serial had to be completed.

12

London

'Doesn't anyone know *anything* about this man?'

The Director pushed aside Carswell's file and looked round the table. Anxiety and frustration had made his voice petulant, and he fidgeted irritably with his gold pencil.

Handley-Reid watched him for a moment with distaste.

Then he leant forward. 'Major Fenton probably knows as much as anyone, Director, but I think we've been over everything that might be relevant—'

'What we've learned so far, Colonel, has got us precisely nowhere,' the Director said. 'If we're going to find him before any—accident—happens, then we've got to know what he's likely to be doing. Only, no one seems able to tell me a damn thing about him—'

He swung round to face Fenton at the far end of the table.

'All right, Major Fenton, he's one of your people—what the hell's he up to?'

Fenton scratched at one of the grey side-burns that straggled down to the corners of his mouth.

'Unfortunately, Director, it's twelve years since I've had any contact with him.' Fenton's teeth showed yellow and hollowed between his lips as he spoke. 'What we're really left with is his war record, which of course seems to have led to this. However—'

He began to go over Carswell's career, trying to amplify the sparse information in the folder.

It was Monday morning, a week after LeKahn had been killed. The Director had called the meeting as soon as Handley-Reid had come down to his office and told him what appeared to have happened to the Robespierre serial's coda. For Handley-Reid the past week had been among the worst he remembered.

For the first few days he hadn't been unduly worried over Carswell's failure to contact Spencer. In the confusion following the Belgian's death, Carswell had probably been unable to reach a telephone. Then on Wednesday Vavasseur had called him. A report in the Madrid daily *ABC* had said two bodies had been found in the posada. One of them was the manager; the other an unidentified foreigner whose companion, a dark-haired girl, according to the maid, had vanished that night.

Had Handley-Reid's sources suggested LeKahn wasn't travelling alone, and that apart from the girl he had someone else with him?

Handley-Reid had expressed immediate bewilderment, said he'd check with the Middle Eastern sections and call Vavasseur back. As soon as he rang off, he asked Fenton to contact the Madrid resident, Garcia.

Garcia reported back the same evening. The police were searching for a group of three people: the girl, a man described as an "Oriental" and another man, who'd rented a room in the village. The first two were foreigners; the third was thought to be a Spaniard. From the police description Garcia had little doubt that the "Spaniard" was Carswell.

Handley-Reid returned Vavasseur's call the next day. He said there'd been no report of an accomplice working with LeKahn, and the girl was believed to be travelling with him solely as cover. All he could guess, Handley-Reid added, was that she'd panicked when she found LeKahn's body, believed she'd be thought responsible for his murder and had somehow killed the manager while she was getting away. Since then she'd presumably been hiding in the hills.

The explanation seemed to satisfy Vavasseur, and the following day the first of the Foreign Office intelligence analysts had flown out to interview Samir.

Thursday and Friday passed with still no word from Carswell. By Saturday Handley-Reid was baffled and worried. Then, at a meeting that afternoon with Cazenove and Mather, Fenton finally came up with what seemed to be the explanation. He'd been glancing through the brief which had been sent to Madrid, when he stopped and looked up frowning.

'I got this right, didn't I, Charles?' Fenton was holding the one-page copy of his memo to Garcia. 'About the way you were running the whole mission—?'

'How do you mean?'

'Well, that evening you came down to see me about Carswell you said you were doing it on a war rules basis. Right?'

'Absolutely.' Handley-Reid nodded. 'It was the obvious way. We'd got a trained operative and I wanted the field-work as simple as possible. Why?'

'Because that's how I told Garcia to brief him.'

'Fine. No doubt he did—'

Handley-Reid broke off suddenly and sat for a moment in silence.

Then he said, 'Christ!'

Fenton tugged at one of his side-burns while Cazenove glanced, puzzled, from one to the other. It was several seconds before he also understood. When he did he whistled sharply.

The war rules. Handley-Reid started to swear, silently at first and then out loud, with the same violent embittered anger which had charged him when the little Arab failed to keep the rendezvous in Geneva. By Monday he decided he'd no choice but to inform the Director.

'If I understand the situation—'

The Director rolled his pencil away as Fenton lamely finished his summary of Carswell's career.

'We're faced with what I believe in the animal world is called a "maverick." In this case an operative who's misinterpreted the function of the mission he was assigned to, may well know where Samir is and is probably making preparations to terminate him—'

He turned towards Handley-Reid.

'It's intolerable, Colonel, intolerable. I'm not interested in the whys and wherefores. I want this man found and stopped. If he's not, we'll have an incident on our hands that'll make Philby look like a missing coffee-break memo.'

'Yes, Director—'

Handley-Reid nodded. The Director's face was white and he was breathing quickly. His voice was still querulous but the sudden outburst of anger had given him an authority he'd never had before.

'We've been working on contingency procedures,' Handley-Reid continued. 'The Spanish police are the first possibility. Through our resident there we can feed them enough information to have the search transferred south, even a photograph to allow them a full identification—'

He glanced at Fenton, who nodded.

'I'm afraid it'll mean disowning any responsibility for him—'

'I don't care a damn what it means,' the Director interrupted. 'Just find him and stop him. When does the Cairo conference start?'

'May 27, Director. That's ten days from now.'

'Well, I'm not having some eleventh-hour drama either. I want this man traced within the next week. That at least will give us three days' grace. Is that clear?'

'Yes, sir.'

The Director stood up and walked out. The others waited in silence for a moment. Then one by one they filed out behind him.

13

Sevilla

Carswell woke to the smell of coffee. Minette was sitting on the end of the bed with a tray between them.

He sat up blinking. 'What's the time—?'

Fumbling for his watch he saw it was nine o'clock. Minette must have drawn the blinds; the clock over the jeweller's outside the window had vanished and the floor was barred with sunlight. He'd slept for twelve hours.

'How did that get there?'

Carswell pointed at the tray and she laughed.

'I ordered it—coffee sounds the same anywhere.'

She poured him a cup and passed it across the bed. There was a pile of toast and a plate of green figs beside the jug. Carswell began to eat hungrily.

'What about you?' he asked.

'Oh, I've been up an hour. I've eaten, showered, all manner of things.'

'That's why you're so pleased with yourself?'

He watched her over the cup. Minette had smiled at him twice, maybe three times during the journey through the mountains; each time quickly and cautiously and always without laughter afterwards.

Now, sitting on the bed with a towel knotted round her, her hair brushed so that it hung straight and thick onto her shoulders and her face fuller again after sleep, the dark eye-shadows and the tight lines of strain gone, she looked a different person.

'Come on, why the hell not?' She shrugged, laughing again. 'How long was it? A week? A whole bloody awful horrible week! All that walking and climbing and rocks and blistering fucking sun and wind and cold, Christ! And now this—'

She stretched out her arm round the room, which was large and clean and cool, with a stone-tiled floor, white-washed walls and a great brass bedstead that gleamed in the morning light.

'That's enough to make anyone feel better—halfway better, anyway. Isn't it?'

'All right—'

Carswell grinned. Then he put down his cup and swung his legs onto the floor.

'Here, let's have a look at your feet.'

Minette moved the tray, turned onto her stomach and lay across the bed with her feet in his lap.

She'd washed off the blood but they were still stained almost black from the juice of the juniper berries. The boil on her ankle had burst and although her leg was red and hot, it was less swollen than before. Most of the raw patches were inflamed and both her soles were serrated with cuts, but on the whole, Carswell decided, it might have been worse. None of the sores were infected and with the right treatment both feet should heal in a few days.

'You'll do,' he said. 'In a moment I'll go out and get some things from a chemist. Then give them a week and they'll be so hard you won't even need shoes.'

He lifted her feet off his lap and was starting to stand up when she twisted her head round, looked at him steadily for a moment, then stretched out her arm.

'Come here, Carswell.'

She caught hold of his wrist and pulled him towards her.

'Minette, listen—'

'Don't tell me to listen any more. Just come here.'

Caught off balance as he tried to stand, Carswell toppled forwards beside her.

She began to kiss him. Slowly at first. Then faster and harder, twisting her body and rubbing it against his as the quilt dropped to the floor. Carswell struggled for a moment. Then he felt desire coming, rising, hardening. He shivered. After so long everything seemed to be snapping painfully inside him, like wakening stiffly after lying out in the damp and feeling muscles crack as they came back to life.

He touched her, felt her breasts, her ribs, the long line of her legs. Then, ravenous, he was on top of her, binding tightly to her, bearing down and moving as she moaned and her head fell back, open-mouthed and panting.

Afterwards he must have dozed off again. When he opened his eyes she was lying curled against him and her shoulders were shaking with laughter.

'What are you laughing at?'

'Because that's the other half of the way to feel better, because I'm laughing and because—'

She broke off, raised her head to look at him and laughed again.

'Oh, Carswell, you think I was laughing at you? I was laughing because I was laughing, that's all.'

'How do you know my name?'

'Saw it there—'

She pointed at his passport on the chair. Carswell had written her first name in the box provided for the bearer's wife, in case the hotel manager had asked for identification. It hadn't been necessary. The manager had taken him for a Spaniard and Carswell had merely signed the register.

'I've had enough of "Jeans" for a while, so I thought I'd call you by the other one,' she said. 'So what do we do now?'

'Rest for a day or two. Then I've got to find out if the person Jean was looking for is really here. If he is, I've got to see him. Afterwards—'

'*See* him?'

'Yes—'

'Don't lie, Carswell. Okay, maybe you had to at the beginning. Not now, not any longer.'

Carswell said nothing. He lay on his back watching the movement of the sunlight on the ceiling as the blinds stirred.

'Know what I think you're like?' Minette's cheek moved against his shoulder as she smiled. 'A nut, that's what. Chestnut, maybe, like the ones you buy off the street-sellers in winter. All hard and brown on the skin and most of the way through too, except sometimes there's a bit right in the middle that's still yellow and sweet.'

She nipped his arm with her teeth. 'See—I was right, wasn't I? Even tastes good. Comes of knowing. Here, know how many men I've had?'

'No, of course I don't.'

'Guess!'

Carswell laughed. 'How could I possibly guess, Minette?'

'Tried to count once. Couldn't get it exactly, but over two hundred.' The number obviously pleased her, because she smiled again. 'Not bad, is it? There's a hell of a lot of money in it too; only those bastards like Julio take it all—'

He remembered Julio was the name of the Corsican she'd left to live with LeKahn.

'Anyway,' Minette went on, 'they talk afterwards, mostly they do. You got to give them half an hour for the money. Well, leaves quite a bit of time if they come quick, doesn't it? So they talk and I listen and you learn all sorts of things.'

'But I haven't talked to you.'

'Don't have to, do you? That's what I was saying, like I know already. You think I'm stupid, the way I talk and that. Well, not nearly so much as you think. I know a lot about men, knew a lot about Jean, know a lot about you too.'

Carswell smiled. 'That I'm a chestnut?'

'Right.' She nodded. 'Jean was one as well, only he was all

hard, right, right to the centre. You're not. That's why I said before, back in the hills, you were different. But you're still going to kill someone, aren't you?'

'Maybe.'

'What did he do to you both? Was there some business that went wrong, that he cheated you in?'

'No, it's not like that.'

'Tell you what I think—'

Minette pushed herself back until her head was resting against the brass bed-rail.

'If it's not business, I think you work for the ministry, you know like for the government or something. They want this man killed, so they paid Jean to do it. Now there's no Jean, you've got to do it yourself. So to you it's just work because it's work, while for Jean it was work because it was money. Only—'

She leant over and ruffled his hair.

'You're not really so good as Jean, are you? All dried up 'til you get to that yellow bit in the middle. Then you have to think and you get muddled. Right?'

'Minette!' Carswell spread out his hands. 'I honestly don't know. Yes, I work for what you call the ministry. And, yes, you've got most of the rest about right too. But whether Jean could have done it and I can't, well, that's something we'll just have to see.'

'I don't have to wait and see,' she said confidently. 'I know. Anyway, I'm going to the bidet.'

Half an hour later Minette was back in bed, leafing through some old picture magazines piled on the bedside table. Carswell had washed, dressed and was ready to go out. Before he left he sat down beside her.

'I'm going to the chemist first,' he said. 'Then there are some other things I want. I'll be out for about an hour, maybe less, certainly no more. I'm almost sure we're safe here, but I can't be sure. So listen carefully—'

Carswell had worked out the procedure while he was shaving. Whenever he went out alone he'd give her the latest time at which he'd be back. If he hadn't returned by then, even if he was a few minutes late, she was to leave the hotel and cross the street to a café on the other side.

Minette was to wait there exactly an hour. If he still hadn't arrived by the end of the hour, she was to take a taxi to the country bus terminal just outside the city on the Córdoba road. There was a café in the terminal—Carswell remembered it from an earlier trip to Sevilla—and she was to spend another hour there. Finally, if he still hadn't joined her, she was to take the next coach to Algeciras.

From Algeciras, four hours down the coast, there were ferries three times a day to Tangier. She'd have his passport, with her name inside as his wife, and he gave her enough money for a ticket on one of the Air France flights from Tangier to Paris. After Paris she'd have to make her own way back to Marseilles.

If anything happened to him while he was out, the chances of her even reaching Algeciras were remote, but it was the best he'd been able to come up with. With any luck the plan wouldn't be necessary. The police hunt would still be concentrated in the north and probably moving closer to the French border. Minette's appearance had been changed dramatically by her blond hair and his own description would be imprecise at most. There was nothing to connect either of them with a double murder five hundred miles away in the Guadalajara mountains.

'Go through it again—'

Carswell listened while she repeated the instructions for the third time.

'All right,' he said. 'Anything you're not sure about?'

Minette shook her head. 'That's fine. But what about you?'

'Me?'

She grinned. 'Maybe soon as you're out of the door I'll just do it anyway.'

'I'll chance it.' Carswell laughed. 'But if you do, leave me the cigarettes!'

Carswell was back well within the time he'd told Minette.

He dressed her feet, using antibiotics and gauze, ordered lunch to be sent up to their room and then, when they'd eaten, settled down by the window while Minette slept again.

Apart from the medical supplies, he'd bought all the newspapers, two maps and a small pamphlet on the Coto Doñana put out by the local tourist office. Carswell read the papers first. There was nothing of interest in the provincial press, but he found a short paragraph at the back of the Madrid daily *ABC* which reported that the hunt for the posada murderers was continuing near Barcelona.

Then he turned to the pamphlet on the Coto. Carswell had never been there, in spite of the many visits he'd made to Sevilla, and the pamphlet added little to what he already knew. The *marismas* themselves, the vast basin of tidal marshland at the mouth of the Guadalquivir River, covered more than a thousand square miles. The Coto—an old Spanish word for a hunting forest—was at the centre of the marshes on the far bank of the river.

An enclave of twenty thousand acres, for centuries it had been Spain's greatest hunting preserve. Then, fifteen years before, it was bought by the World Wildlife Fund and turned into a rigorously protected sanctuary for the teeming birds and animals of the marshes. Fenced on the inland sides, patrolled by mounted rangers and still supporting a few scattered hamlets of farmers and fishermen, the whole area was dominated by the *palacio* of the Doña Ana who'd given the Coto its name.

A large, rugged sprawling building, more like a fortress than a palace, the *palacio* had been built as a hunting lodge in the sixteenth century and used by the Spanish kings who'd come to the Coto to shoot. Now it housed the Wildlife Fund's research station, with one wing kept available for the rare visitor to the preserve, whose trip had to be arranged months in advance through the Coto's director general.

Most of that Carswell remembered from what he'd read before. What interested him now were the pamphlet's photographs of the *palacio* and the surrounding landscape. The more he studied them, the more convinced he became that LeKahn's guess was right. It would have been simple for the Americans to rent the entire visitors' wing, probably in the guise of a massive donation to the Fund's constantly overtaxed resources.

Once they'd done that and moved in Samir with his entourage, they'd have created the ideal sanctuary. Supplementing the Coto's mounted rangers with their own guards, they'd have made it virtually impossible for any stranger to approach within a mile of the Arab without being detected. At least that was what it looked like from the maps which Carswell opened next.

To reach the *palacio* he could try either to cross the Coto from the inland side or to approach it from the river. The first was out of the question; the distance was too great and he'd inevitably be discovered before he was half a mile beyond the fences. The only possibility was the Guadalquivir River.

The *palacio* was set back two hundred yards from the river's edge. If he could cross at night, which almost certainly meant swimming, he might be able to find a hiding-place before daylight and lie up there until he'd finally established that Samir was in the building.

Afterwards, he could start working out how to accomplish the last stage of the mission.

Carswell folded the maps and walked over to the bed.

'Come on.' He tugged at Minette's ear. 'Time to get dressed. I want to take you out and get you some new clothes—'

'Clothes? For real?' She sat up instantly, her face alight with pleasure. 'You mean now?'

Carswell laughed. 'Don't get carried away. We're not shopping for a trousseau. I just want you to have something less noticeable than those—'

He pointed at the silver-studded jeans, torn and stained now, which she'd worn ever since they left the posada.

'Maybe some shoes too, since there's not much left of the sandals—'

She jumped out of bed before he'd finished speaking and ran to the bathroom.

For Carswell there was something unreal about the rest of that day and the next, the sense of a space set apart from time.

Partly it was reaction. They'd arrived at the hotel exhausted, drained in mind and body by the days of travel along the ridges, the snatched hours of sleep, the hurried meals, the constant tension of watching for the search parties. Now, in the gathering heat as Sevilla pivoted from spring to summer, life came flooding back.

The room was quiet, hazy with warmth by day as the bars of sunlight filtered through the blinds, cool and airy at night. No one came there except a white-headed maid who smiled gravely as she made the bed at morning and evening. Outside, the streets smelt of smoke from the charcoal braziers of the *pinchito* stalls, smoke and river-smells and oranges ripening on the trees that lined every square. At dusk the last of the water-carts would rumble by, leaving the air clean and dust-free, and twice Carswell woke at dawn to hear the slow clatter of hoofs on the roadway below.

Yet it wasn't only reaction to that night in the posada, with LeKahn's blood staining the bed-spread and the limp huddle of the manager's body by the stairs; or just returning strength after the week in the hills. The rest, the feeling of strangeness and difference, was due to Minette.

The first evening they went to a department store a few blocks from the hotel. Inside she was like a child, making Carswell stand with her in the changing booth while she tried on dress after dress, or dragging him behind her as she riffled delightedly through rows of blouses.

'Minette—!'

He was hanging up something she'd just discarded when he turned round to find the booth door open. Outside Minette was searching unconcernedly and almost naked through the racks. The sales girls were gazing at her in amazement and people were turning round at the other end of the store.

'For Christ's sake!' He pulled her inside and shut the door. 'This isn't the south of France. It's deep Andalucía, which means about two hundred years back. They call the police here if you do things like that.'

'What the hell do they think'll happen? Someone's going to see my boobs and start a revolution—?'

She doubled over with laughter. Then she pressed herself against him.

'All right, Carswell, only let's make it a private one right here!'

'Minette, please—'

She'd stepped out of her underclothes and was trying to unbuckle his belt.

'Why not? Christ, you're so fucking inhibited, that's your problem—all tied up in little knots. Come on! You're getting it for free; other fellows have to come with the wallet first.'

Eventually she bought two pairs of jeans, a matching jacket, some shoes, several blouses and, at Carswell's insistence, light-weight rubber-soled boots.

'Where now?'

Minette had run ahead of him into the street. In her new clothes, her face tanned and laughing, her tawny hair shaking out in the evening breeze, it was impossible to connect her with the sullen white-cheeked girl who'd reached out of LeKahn's car and clawed savagely at his skin.

'Food.'

Carswell caught up with her, linked his arm through hers and they set off towards the old quarter of the town.

They had dinner in a small restaurant near the Barrio de Santa Cruz. There was a large patio at the back, open to the sky and heavy with the scent of jasmine, and the tables were lit by candles set in bowls of flowers. Carswell ordered platters of grilled prawns, rose-coloured and crusted with salt, and then roast quail shot out of season in the hills to the west. The waiter brought an earthenware jug of the rough red wine of Rioja and, after they'd eaten, small cups of black coffee.

'Know what this is—'

Minette laughed. It was dark by then, the sky bright with stars, and lanterns had been lit in the jasmine branches.

'My holiday! The one I thought that creep was taking me on and wasn't. It is now. Know what? It's even better than I thought the first one'd be—'

She paused. Carswell had only been half listening to her. He must have been frowning, because she leant forward suddenly and shook his wrist.

'Hey, what's the matter? Like I said, it's a holiday, should be one for you too. I mean, you're not paying, are you?'

He shook his head. 'No, I was just thinking—'

'Thinking? What about? That other fellow or me?'

'Neither.' Carswell smiled. 'Although I might well have been thinking about you. A few days ago you were hell-bent on removing most of the skin from my face. Then, when that didn't work, you had a go at rearranging me in *brochettes* with a broken bottle—'

'*Bon dieu!*'

Minette cut him off and threw her head back in exasperation.

'That was last week! Christ, you got all the words but you don't know *nothing* about women, do you, Carswell?' She laughed again. 'How long since you last had one?'

'Quite a time.'

'I knew it! And how much did you get hustled?'

'About thirty francs.'

'Thirty francs?' Her voice was scornful. 'Must have been a real scrubber!'

'Well, it was some while ago and it wasn't France and then there's been inflation—'

Carswell broke off, laughing at himself now. It had been in Madrid. He used to go to the brothels off the Avenida Quiepo de Llano for a year or so after he'd been sent there.

The girls were mainly gypsies, young, dark-skinned, sloe-eyed, often very beautiful. He'd pay before he went into one of the cubicles and afterwards, if the evening was quiet, he'd stay there for several hours talking and drinking as the rest of their families drifted in.

Then he'd stopped going. There was no particular reason but his visits had tailed off, and it must have been six years since he'd been there last. Somehow it had been part of the general falling-off of his contacts with other people. All that was left now were the games of chess with Ramón and the occasional dinner with the resident.

'Christ, scrubbers like that, it's no wonder, is it?' Minette took his wrist again. 'Want to know about women, Carswell, really know about them?'

'Well, as I've learned about men,' he said, chuckling, 'maybe I'd better have my education completed.'

'Makers-do and menders, that's what we are, all of us, whores or whatever. We patch things up, make something out of scraps, out of anything you pricks leave behind. Just so it's enough to live off. That's why I'm here now—and happy with it. No reason, nothing sinister, just because I can make it work—'

Her mouth had been bulging with fruit as she spoke. Now she took a cigarette, lit it and blew the smoke across the table.

'Jesus, Carswell, not because it's you. Could be you, could be Jean, could be whoever. You all make fucking great pigs' dinners out of things and we come behind and then while you're dreaming about the next thing that isn't going to be a cock-up, we pick up the pieces of the last one and cobble them together. Cobble them into something that works. That's the point, that it works. If it does, then you can be happy—'

She shook her head.

'Look, what could I do? Back there after you'd conned me to come with you. Fight you all the way? Or make the best of it, stitch it up and live with it, even have fun? Well, that's what I did and don't tell me you don't like it.'

'I'm not, Minette.'

'Only, it's still funny to you, isn't it?'

'In a way, yes.'

'A wife and thirty-franc scrubbers!' She snorted contemptuously. 'Explains everything, doesn't it? So what was she like then, your old lady?'

Carswell told her later. They'd gone back to the hotel and he'd taken down the leather case he'd removed from LeKahn's room. He hadn't opened it until then. There'd been no need; Carswell knew what it contained and there wasn't time on the walk through the mountains to pick the solid Yale lock that bonded the lid to the frame.

Minette lay in bed watching him as he sat by the window with the case on his knee.

'I wasn't with her long,' Carswell said. 'We got married when I was in the army. Then I had to go away for a time. And in the end she went off with someone else.'

It was a trivial story. In a way that bald summary said everything there was to say about it. In fact so much time had passed since, that remembering what had happened needed a conscious effort now.

Carswell had married her a few months after he'd been commissioned. It had lasted exactly a year; five months to her first lover, seven more to the final one and it was over. The Korean war had started by then. He did his first six-month tour near Seoul and came back for two weeks' leave. There'd been no answer to his cable and he arrived the day she was moving out.

It was late afternoon, October, with the light going and leaves falling in the mist which covered the street. There were packing cases in the hall and two men carrying out the furniture they'd been given as wedding presents. Carswell came in as she was walking downstairs. She must have been packing all day, because she looked tired. For a moment she thought he was another removal man and she asked him to collect the cooker from the kitchen. Then she saw his uniform.

'Oh, it's you,' she said. 'I wondered when you'd get back. I'm just clearing the last—'

She stopped as she saw him looking up at her from the doorway in bewilderment.

'You got my letter, didn't you?' she said.

Carswell shook his head.

'Oh hell!' She paused again, momentarily confused. Then she went on quickly, 'I'm going. I don't want to talk about it, the letter explains everything—whatever there is to explain. Only now you're here, you might as well help with the last few things. I've still got a lot to do.'

She disappeared into the kitchen.

Carswell had flown for nineteen hours. Apart from anything else, he was tired. He didn't help the removal men. Instead he went into the sitting-room. All the chairs had gone but the wall-cabinet was still there with a half-bottle of whiskey inside; it must have been bought for someone else, since he normally didn't drink it. He took several mouthfuls, sat down on the floor and waited. An hour later he heard her tipping the men. Then she looked in, said good-bye and a moment afterwards the door-latch clicked.

He stood up and walked slowly round the house. A few of his own possessions—some books, a collection of records, two suits, his citation for the Légion d'honneur (he'd lost the cross the French embassy had sent him)—had been piled in the landing bathroom. Apart from that everything had been taken, literally everything—even the light bulbs had gone.

Carswell slept that night in the hall on a roll of underfelt which had been accidentally left behind. The divorce took a further year and a half to come through. By then he was back in Korea.

'Well, that was easy for her to do, wasn't it?' Minette shrugged. 'I mean, she had money, didn't she? Must have done to have all those things. Maybe her new fellow was coining it too. Lucky, she was, that's what I'd say—dead lucky.'

'Looked at like that, I suppose she was.'

Carswell smiled. He'd opened LeKahn's case, removed the gun and was starting to assemble it.

The weapon was a high-velocity Mannlicher automatic rifle. LeKahn had had it modified in such a way that the whole gun could be broken down into sections under two feet long. Even the heavy teak stock had been stripped and cut into halves, with a sunken bolt that locked them together again. There were boxes of bullets fitted into a recess in the base and a special velvet-lined compartment holding a McConnell-Yamaha telescopic sight.

It was a superb piece of workmanship. After a while Carswell found he could put it together in under three minutes.

'Think that's unkind, don't you—?'

Minette had seen him smiling across the room at her last remark.

'You're wrong. It's not, just the way things are. She had a choice so she went with someone else. I didn't so I went with Jean, like now I'm with you. It's the same, we make it work whoever we're with. You understand that, you take it like it is, then you're fine. If you don't, then you can get bad inside. Maybe that's why you're all dried up.'

'Maybe.'

'What about the rest? What about this thing you're doing now?'

'Well, I suppose that started when I was a soldier. It really began before, but this part when I went back later—'

Carswell had returned to Korea forty-eight hours after he'd arrived in London, forgoing the rest of his leave and rejoining his unit immediately.

They were moved north towards the parallel a week later. Afterwards there were months of front-line fighting, months of mud and night patrols and lines of tracer in the darkness, months of struggling to win some bald rain-sodden hillock, holding it for days against the human-wave attacks of the North Korean militia, yielding it to them and then returning across the black cratered earth to battle for it again.

Finally, in the early spring, there'd been Heartbreak Ridge. A craggy barren stretch of rock, shale and shattered tree-stumps which the North Koreans had fortified as their last key defensive line. Carswell's company—he was a captain by then—had been part of the task force spearheading the assault on the ridge's western sector. Three days after the attack was launched one of his platoon commanders, a white-faced exhausted boy of eighteen, crawled over to the company command post and told Carswell that a member of the platoon was refusing to move forward from the trench where they were grouped.

Carswell crawled back to the trench with him. It was a shallow water-filled ditch on a foothill before the ridge. He ordered the rest of the men forward and waited while they ran to a line of cover ahead. Then he began to walk along the ditch towards the one man who still hadn't moved. He was five yards away when the man suddenly raised his rifle, worked the bolt and swung towards him.

Carswell didn't even have time to shout. There was a deafening crack as the man fired, a billow of grey smoke, the stench of cordite, then the sound of the bolt sliding forward again.

Carswell threw himself to one side, pulled out his revolver and squeezed the trigger until the magazine was empty, aiming blindly through the smoke. One of the shots must have found its target because as the smoke cleared he saw the man toppling slowly onto his face.

A moment later, before he was even sure the man was dead, there was a prolonged volley of small-arms fire close to the ditch and the detonations of exploding grenades. Then, screaming and running, the men he'd sent forward a few minutes earlier began to throw themselves back on top of him. They'd advanced just as the Koreans had mounted a massive counter-attack, and the first assault waves had hit them seconds after they'd reached the cover ahead.

Carswell managed to rally them in the ditch, but the offensive was too sudden and too concentrated to be contained there. He held the position as long as he could, then he pulled the platoon back and eventually regrouped it with the rest of the company half a mile from where they'd started.

'And that was the end of my being a soldier,' he said. 'Well, not quite the end. They had a court of inquiry afterwards; only the trouble was no one knew what had really happened—not even me. So they decided I wasn't quite wrong but I wasn't quite right, and to balance it out they sent me back to a camp a long way from the fighting.'

'So you left the army?' Minette said

Carswell nodded. 'I could have gone on, I suppose. But there'd always have been a large question-mark against my name. You see, while you're told to do what I did if one of your soldiers won't obey orders—let alone if he tries to shoot you first—it's rather different when it actually happens. Then it's not very nice; it becomes embarrassing and the papers might hear about it and so on. So it's much easier if they tidy you away.'

'But why join the ministry?'

'The ministry?' Carswell laughed. 'All right, Minette, it's

not quite like what you think, but maybe that's as good a word as any—'

He dismantled the rifle and started to fit the pieces back into the leather case.

'I didn't really join it, better to say I went back to it. I'd worked for them before, in the big war, when I was very young. And they'd kept their word always. Not like being married, not like the army. They were people you could trust. So after I found out the rest of the world wasn't like that, I went back to the one place I knew was safe. And that's where I've been ever since.'

'Safe?' Minette snorted. 'Nowhere's safe, nowhere except what you make for yourself—'

Carswell closed the gun-case and put it back on top of the cupboard. In the distance the cathedral clock was chiming midnight.

'No, that's not quite true,' Minette added. 'Sometimes you get given things and they're safe only you don't see it, I mean people like you. You think safe things are for always and that if they're not for always, then they're not safe—'

She laughed and stretched out her hand.

'Come to bed, Carswell. That's safe. Me, I'm safe too. You hang onto that, worth having while it lasts. Christ, better than sleeping alone like a dried-up old chestnut, isn't it?'

He got into bed. Minette was still laughing softly when he went to sleep.

14

Coto Doñana

Carswell left for the Coto in the afternoon of the third day after they'd arrived in Sevilla.

That morning he bought a pair of swimming fins and a length of oil-cloth which Minette fashioned into a rough bag. Inside he packed a pair of binoculars he'd borrowed from the desk clerk, a straw-covered water-bottle and enough food to last him through the thirty-six hours he guessed he'd be away. He told Minette to wait until midday on the day after the next. If he hadn't returned by then, she was to go through the procedure he'd worked out the first evening.

'Don't worry,' she said. 'Just you come back, Carswell, I'll be here.'

The room was littered with her belongings; a pair of jeans on the floor, underclothes washed and spread out to dry on the window sill, shoes—she'd made him buy her two more pairs—lying in a heap by the cupboard, the scent LeKahn had given her hanging on the warm afternoon air.

Carswell took a taxi to the bus station, then a coach south towards Cádiz. Two hours later he got out at the little town of Benalmartín. The Guadalquivir was half a mile beyond the town. From the map it looked as if the *palacio* was directly opposite on the other bank; the width of the river there would depend on the year's rainfall and the strength of the tidal run that night.

Carswell walked through the town in the early dusk, reached the edge of the estuary and turned right along the sandy bank. On the far side, almost a mile across the water, the Coto looked grey and sultry; there were some low pine trees, a line of sand dunes and a few wedges of reed reaching out into the stream. He found a muddy inlet, sat down in the thick grass and waited until dark. At ten he undressed, packed his clothes in the oilskin bag, put on the fins and waded into the water. It was chillingly cold after the heat and dust of the shore; the Atlantic currents obviously swept far up the estuary, carrying with them deep-sea water from the ocean beyond the river mouth. Gasping, he struck out for the other side.

The crossing took over an hour. At the start the stream was slack and he needed only twenty minutes to reach the centre of the river. Then the tide began to run and the current started to push him back. He kicked out more strongly but there were long periods when he thought he'd have to give up. It was only when the water started to become warmer and he realized he was approaching the far shore that he knew he'd succeeded.

Soon there was mud under his feet again. Carswell eased himself forward into an arrow of reed, lay there until he'd recovered his wind and slowly stood up.

'*Cuanto mas?*'

The voice came from somewhere to his left. Carswell froze and lowered himself back into the reeds. Then he heard another voice.

'*No se. Dos o tres creo.*'

The second speaker was even closer than the first, perhaps fifteen yards away. Carswell lifted his head cautiously.

On either side of him a series of lines a few yards apart ran down over the mud into the water. They were night cray-fish lines; the voices belonged to a couple of fishermen checking them before they went to bed. The silhouette of a head and shoulders appeared on the bank and Carswell guessed why he hadn't been seen; the fishermen were crouched down, shuffling on their haunches from line to line, and he'd been swimming directly before the rising moon. In the dazzle of light on the water his movements must have looked like wind ripples.

He flattened himself into the reeds, pressing his face against the damp sand, praying they hadn't got a dog; the nearest line was only a few feet from where he was lying. The fishermen shuffled forward, water splashed as the lines were pulled in, a fish flapped glistening on the mud, tobacco smoke drifted through the reeds.

'Bueno, estamos.'

Carswell waited a few moments. Then he lifted his head and peered up the shore.

The fishermen were walking away up the bank, wicker creels swinging from their waists and the ends of their cigarettes tracing patterns against the sky. They turned inland and disappeared into the darkness through the scrub and pines that ran down to the estuary shore.

He gave them five minutes before he crawled forward to the trees and dressed. Then he tried to work out where he was. It was much more difficult than he'd imagined. The *palacio* should be about half a mile to his right as he looked inland. On the other hand if the current had swept him upstream, it might well be behind him to his left. In that case he could walk northwards all night and by morning simply find himself lost somewhere in the heart of the *marismas*.

The smell reached him as he stood searching for a landmark on the far shore; a strong rich fragrance carried down from the north on the light wind. Carswell sniffed and recognized it instantly; crushed wild rosemary. Then he guessed what had caused it; the two fishermen had trampled a path between the bushes and the scent was coming from the broken branches.

Providing he was anywhere near the *palacio*, the chances were that the fishermen came from the little settlement beside it. If he followed the trail of the scent, it should bring him straight to the building. He picked up his oilskin bag and set off along the shore, turning into the scrub where the footprints led away from the mud.

He walked for half an hour. Several times he lost the trail but always, after casting round in circles through the bushes, he picked it up again. Then, just as he was starting to think the men were heading for another more distant hamlet, he saw the lights ahead of him, six of them shining in two rows through the darkness. He slowed down and worked his way cautiously forward.

Behind the lights was a line of tall eucalyptus; he remembered them from the photograph and he could see them clearly against the sky—the trees round the *palacio*. As far as he could tell, the building was surrounded by open plain, interspersed with great patches of scrub and the occasional towering tree—the nesting sites of colonies of white storks. He could check the details of the landscape with daylight; the immediate problem was to find somewhere to hide before the sun rose.

He walked back to a small thicket he'd passed earlier, crawled into its centre along a narrow tunnel between the thorns, sat down and lit a cigarette. The idea came to him when he tried to stand and his head struck a tangle of branches so dense they felt like a spiney mattress. Crouching, Carswell twisted his neck to look up. The branches had woven themselves together into a solid roof, with only a few scraps of sky showing. He took out his knife and started to hack a hole close to the main trunk.

An hour later he was lying on his stomach ten feet above the ground. The branches didn't stop there but they thinned out considerably, and it took him only a further twenty minutes to carve a small chamber where he could sit upright. Finally, he cut a passage through to the outer wall of the thicket and opened a gap in the leaves. Looking through, he could see straight across the plain to the *palacio*. All the lights apart from one had been turned out.

Carswell climbed back to the ground, crawled out through

the tunnel and sliced off an armful of branches from a cluster of young rosemary bushes. He crushed them between his hands until he was enveloped by a cloud of the heavy scent he'd followed from the shore. Then, dragging them behind him like a broom, he walked backwards to the thicket and heaped them across the tunnel entrance. It wouldn't entirely protect him from any dogs which might come nosing around with daylight, but it would certainly confuse them.

It was almost one. Carswell heaved himself back to the platform. He was sweating in spite of the night air, the thorns had gashed his skin and the little chamber was painfully cramped—a subway telephone booth like those in which he'd spent so many hours waiting over the years, except this one was laid on its side and bristling with spikes. He smiled. At least he was halfway there: he'd crossed into the Coto and found a place from where he could watch the *palacio* when day came.

Leaning back against the trunk, he settled down to wait for dawn.

He must have fallen asleep, because he sat up suddenly and saw a circle of grey light in front of him. Stiff and bleary-eyed, Carswell eased himself forward and looked out. For a moment he couldn't think what had happened; the plain stretched away in front, wet and glittering with dew, and the sky was already filling with light, turning from a pale green to pink and then gold. But there was nothing else at all; the *palacio* had vanished, so had the dark line of the eucalyptus; even the wedge of pine trees he rememberd to the right had disappeared.

Then he realized it was mist. A coil lifted, he saw the crown of the trees, then the whiteness drifted back. Seconds afterwards he heard a diesel engine. It seemed to come out from behind the building, drive round to the front and stop. Another followed, then a third. Later a horse neighed and there was the distant clatter of hoofs on stone. The sky grew paler and the rim of the sun lifted in the east.

The cavalcade appeared at exactly half past six. Carswell heard the engines again, all three of them coughing to life and coming closer in the still-dense greyness that blotted out everything more than fifty yards from the thicket. He saw the horses first, advancing slowly through the mist with their riders sitting like mounted soldiers in the high-pommelled Andalucían saddles. The smell of the saddle oil came to him as the morning wind gusted against the thicket.

He raised the binoculars, focussed and gazed out between the leaves.

There were five horsemen. Samir was riding at the centre of the line, his face half-hooded by the Arab head-dress, his hands neat and precise as he guided his mount, a Spanish thoroughbred stallion, compact, white and powerful, mane and tail flaring, dancing almost sideways as he threaded it through the scrub.

Samir. Carswell lowered the glasses briefly. A great wave of relief and exultation swept over him. He had known so instinctively from the moment the black Ford roared past him in the coastal village five hundred miles to the north. He'd held stubbornly to the conviction ever since. Through the long gruelling hours as he interrogated Minette, on the journey across the mountains, during the days in Sevilla when it had plucked constantly at the back of his mind.

If there'd ever been any doubt, there wasn't any longer. Even half-hooded, even without Carswell's memory of the photograph in the file, the Arab was unmistakeable: the greying beard, the lined olive skin, the pale restless almond eyes, the delicate, almost feminine, features. Carswell rubbed his face, lifted the binoculars and trained them on the procession again.

Two of the other men in the line were dressed like Samir; the fourth, wearing leather chaps and a flat Sevillana hat, was probably one of the Coto rangers; the fifth was obviously an American, a heavy-set man in an open-necked shirt and dark glasses. Behind them came the cars, three Land-Rovers with a pair of guards sitting in the front of each; all of them had rifles across their knees.

Carswell didn't notice the hawks until the riders were almost abreast of the thicket. Then something flapped on Samir's wrist. A large female peregrine falcon was settling itself nervously on his glove, its head covered by a scarlet-embroidered leather hood and the silver bells on its jesses glittering in the early sunlight. The other two Arabs were also carrying hawks and there were more birds on a frame in one of the Land-Rovers. As the procession passed he heard the bells chiming, a fragile metallic sound that echoed above the surf-like churning of the bushes and the clank of the stirrup-irons.

Then both horsemen and cars vanished to the left of his window. Carswell turned and for the next half hour he glimpsed them through other gaps in the leaves. It wasn't difficult to gather what was happening. A mile beyond the thicket the sand dunes started. The Land-Rovers stopped at the edge of the dunes, the riders fanned out, moved slowly forward and halted too. Several minutes afterwards Samir suddenly galloped ahead, with the other horsemen following more slowly behind.

Carswell couldn't see the falcon but Samir had clearly loosed it, probably at a partridge, and was riding towards the kill. He watched as the whole party disappeared behind the dunes.

They rode back at midday. Long before then Carswell discovered it was little short of a miracle he'd reached the thicket at all. First, there were the Coto rangers. At eight a dozen of them, mounted and accompanied by dogs, converged on the *palacio*. Shortly afterwards another twelve rode out from it. An hour later five Land-Rovers appeared in the main courtyard archway, spread out and drove off in different directions; as far as he could tell each one contained five men.

Then at half past nine, as the last of the mist cleared, three figures came out of a door in the left-hand wing of the building. They stood for a time talking and smoking in the sunlight, before walking to positions in the surrounding out-buildings.

As the morning passed he saw others; it was impossible to tell how many, but in total there were probably ten round the *palacio* itself, a further twenty-five in the Land-Rovers and of course the dozen mounted rangers with their dogs.

Carswell put down the binoculars. Somehow he'd evaded all of the night guards. His chances of doing that again were negligible. Even if he did, the problem was still academic. The building itself was clearly impregnable and whenever Samir left it he was escorted by four men on horseback and a further six in the Land-Rovers—all of them never more than fifty yards from him.

There was no remote possibility of Carswell being able to fire a single shot without being found within seconds. Being found, in those circumstances, meant quite simply being gunned down. He smiled as the thought crossed his mind that his body might be an embarrassment to London.

As he reached for a cigarette, he heard the cars again. The line of horsemen was a mile away, where the dunes ran into the plain, with the Land-Rovers churning up fans of sand behind them. Samir was riding slightly in front of the line. As Carswell swung the glasses onto him, the Arab suddenly jerked his wrist upwards.

A partridge had risen from the bushes. Samir's hawk, chest gleaming bars of brown and white, flared up by the horse's head, hung there for a moment, then surged after the partridge. Immediately Samir touched the stallion and galloped forward in pursuit. Carswell glanced away to follow the chase. The two birds, the partridge jinking in front, the hawk steadily overtaking it, were flying directly towards the thicket.

As the hawk climbed higher to stoop, a third bird came into his line of vision. Flying low and fast from the west, a dark arrow-shape against the sky, it was obviously hunting the same prey. For an instant the two predators looked as if they'd collide above the terrified partridge. Then Samir's falcon banked steeply and soared upwards. The other hawk, a marsh harrier, struck viciously at the partridge, missed and flew on out of sight, while the partridge itself skimmed down into the scrub.

'*Na'asr—*'

Carswell heard the shout and glanced back at Samir.

He was a hundred yards in front of the others by then, holding up one hand and waving them back. Carswell watched him ride slowly forward. The falcon was still circling overhead. Samir was less than seventy yards from the thicket when he put the partridge up again. As the bird hurled itself frantically through the air towards the safety of Carswell's hiding-place, the hawk steadied itself, planed down and stooped.

The two met at Carswell's eye-level thirty feet from where he was lying. There was a sharp crack as the hawk's talons hit the partridge's back, an explosion of brown feathers, then both birds tumbled to the ground. The hawk retracted its talons, arched its wings and perched, glaring yellow-eyed over the carcass beneath. At the same instant Carswell felt the branches vibrate with the beat of hoofs and Samir galloped up. The rest of the party was still half a mile behind.

Samir dismounted, gently lifted the falcon, slipped on the scarlet-embroidered hood and waited for the others to arrive. The two Arabs reached him first. As they stopped, Samir held up the dead partridge and pointed at the thicket laughing.

Carswell rocked back into the shadow of the tunnel. The sun was behind him now and he could see Samir's eyes narrow as the Arab looked up. There was sweat on his horse's flanks and the hawk's bells chimed again as it preened itself on his wrist.

Then Samir remounted, they all wheeled and galloped back to the centre of the plain, where they turned towards the *palacio*. Ten minutes later the whole procession disappeared through the archway; long after they'd gone, dust from the wheels of the last Land-Rover was still eddying in the air against the white walls.

15

Castellar de la Frontera

Carswell got back to the hotel at ten the next morning.

While his luck continued to hold, the return journey only confirmed he'd no reasonable chance of repeating it. The distance from the thicket to the river was little more than a mile; it took him the entire night to cover it. Four times he almost walked into one of the mounted guards and once he had to lie motionless for two hours before the horseman moved away.

For some reason, possibly the crushed herbs he'd smeared himself with before he started, the dogs didn't pick up his scent, and at dawn he slipped back into the water. He swam to the other bank on the slack tide, walked through the quiet early-morning fields to the main road and hitched a lift on a fruit truck into Sevilla.

Minette was still asleep when he opened the bedroom door. He closed it softly behind him, sat down in the bedside chair and lit a cigarette. The rasp of the match woke her. She stirred, yawned and opened her eyes.

'See, Carswell, I didn't go—'

She reached out her hand and smiled.

'Know what I did? Waited up 'til fucking four o'clock, case you came back in the night. And I woke up again—twice! What about that, then? Almost thought it was you who wasn't coming back, not me.'

'I nearly didn't,' he said. 'But that's a different story.'

'Find the man you wanted?'

'Yes, he was there, just as Jean guessed.'

'What else?'

Carswell told her: the swim, the walk through the scrub to the thicket, the pattern of Samir's day, the shifts of mounted guards, the Land-Rovers quartering the Coto, the burly men in open-necked shirts round the *palacio* itself.

'Jesus!' Minette was frowning as he finished. 'You can't go back there, can you? I mean, you don't stand a bleeding chance.'

'Not at the moment, no.'

'So—?'

'So I'll think about it.'

'Think about it? What good's that going to do?' She shook her head irritably. 'Look, you don't really have to kill this man, do you, Carswell? Those bosses of yours, that ministry or whatever, they can't make you do it, not if you're going to get hit yourself—'

'If there was a reasonable chance—'

'Chance? Why take a chance, any fucking chance?'

'Because—'

Carswell stopped. He could have produced many reasons: the pattern in which he was only one element, the critical importance of Samir's intelligence, so many more. In the end it was none of those. It was something he'd accepted unconsciously ever since he'd rejoined the Service after Korea, something he'd defined almost accidentally when he'd been talking to Minette before. A matter of trust, of keeping faith.

No one else had kept faith with him. He'd sloughed off the memories, locked them away, his wife, the army, the silent bitterness he'd felt after the court of inquiry, the laughable legal deceit of his divorce. They all belonged to the past and that past was gone—buried and forgotten.

That was what he'd thought. He'd been wrong. Sullen, tawdry, vulnerable and vicious, Minette had suddenly stumbled into the centre of his life. Arrived there and looked round and then, with no other options open, had claimed its territory for herself and pitched camp. Afterwards, talking, laughing, questioning, she'd opened the past again, brought it back—yet brought it back in an utterly different way, because she saw and felt everything so differently herself.

Somehow her presence—vital, calculating, naïve, signed in cheap scent and dirty scattered clothes—had changed everything. Afterwards there'd remained from the past only one fact irrefutable, unalterable. A debt. A debt she'd unwittingly highlighted as she talked. Carswell's debt to the Service.

In the case of the Robespierre serial it required him to complete the mission he'd been entrusted with.

'Maybe, Minette,' he said at last, 'because this time it's different, it's a settling of accounts. And it's over something important enough to take chances.'

'Not hopeless ones?'

'No.'

'Well, tell them this one is,' she said. 'Telephone them, or something. Maybe they'll send someone else, like sending you with Jean.'

'I'll sleep on it first.'

'Fucking crazy.' She shrugged. 'That's what you are—crazy!'

Carswell smiled, stood up stiffly and began to undress. He'd forgotten how tired he was after the night inching down to the river and then the long swim back.

'But what then?' Minette insisted, gripping his arm as he got into bed. 'What if you can't think of anything?'

'Then I'll really have to tell them it's impossible—but I'll come up with something.'

'Crazy, that's what I say, crazy!'

She snorted, moved to the other side of the bed, turned onto her side and went back to sleep.

In spite of his tiredness Carswell lay awake, his mind churning. There were two problems, separate but inextricably interlinked: to get back undetected into the Coto, and then to draw

Samir far enough away from his guards to allow himself a shot with enough time for a chance of escaping afterwards.

He might manage the first. In spite of all the odds, it was just possible he could cross the river and find somewhere like the thicket again without being seen. Yet even if he did, he was still faced with the fact that as soon as he fired he was trapped. The sole tenuous possibility was to create some sort of diversion. But that would require help and help was out of the question; it had been from the moment the cut-out point had come. The girl was useless to him; even if he could cross the Guadalquivir again, it was inconceivable he could take her with him.

He shifted restlessly and reached for a cigarette. Then, as his hand touched the packet, he stopped. Something was tugging at his memory, something that had to do with the tiny township just outside the northern limits of the Coto. He waited a moment, got out of bed, dressed and went downstairs.

The hotel manager was behind the reception counter. He looked up and smiled as Carswell crossed the hall.

'*Buenos dias, señor.*'

'*Buenos dias.*' Carswell slurred his words into the same thick Andalucían dialect. 'Tell me, am I wrong or doesn't the festival of the Rocio happen about now?'

'The Rocio? Of course, *señor,* next Monday. Look—'

He pointed at the wall behind him. Carswell glanced up and saw the poster; a hard-faced wooden Virgin sitting on a golden throne with the words "La Virgen del Rocio" and the date, May 26, beneath her.

Carswell nodded. That was what had reminded him. He must have noticed the poster unconsciously every time he'd been through the hall, and the name together with the image of the Virgin's face had snagged in his mind.

'You've never been, *señor?*' The manager added, 'It is one of the greatest sights of Spain, many people say of the world. Columbus sailed a week late on the voyage when he discovered

America because all his sailors left the ships to go on the pilgrimage that year. Here—'

He pulled out a supplement to the day's edition of the *Diario de Cádiz* and gave it to Carswell.

'It has all the details. The Virgin is carried through Rocio on Monday, but the festival starts when the brotherhoods ride into the marshes to get there. From Sevilla they leave the day after tomorrow, Friday—well, you'll read it all inside.'

'Thank you.' Carswell took the supplement. 'And they ride through the Coto, don't they?'

'They ride from everywhere, through everywhere, *señor.*' The manager smiled again. 'One hundred thousand people coming from all quarters of Spain. They say of the true Rocieros, the pilgrims, that if the gates of hell were built across the marshes, they'd ride through them to be with the Virgin on her day.'

Carswell thanked him and went back upstairs. He slid into bed without waking Minette, opened the paper and began to read.

Six hundred years ago. That was when it was supposed to have started. No one knew for certain; the historical reality, the legend it rapidly became, the myths which grew up over the centuries, all of them had intertwined. The legend was woven round a hunter who'd gone into the marshes one day with his dogs. The dogs had pointed at a thicket, the hunter raised his gun and when nothing came out, he walked forward into the bushes. There, in a small clearing, he found a wooden Virgin—hidden, perhaps, by some villagers centuries earlier to prevent her falling into the hands of the conquering Moors.

He dragged the Virgin out and started to carry her back to his own village, Almonte. After a while the heat made him sleepy and he lay down to rest. When he woke the Virgin had vanished. He cast round and found her again in the clearing where he'd discovered her first. Next day he returned with a group of men from Almonte and they too tried and failed to carry her to the village—falling asleep as he'd done and waking to find the Virgin in the clearing again.

Finally the village priest was called. He pronounced her the Virgin of the marshes, and picked the clearing for her shrine. So they built a church to protect her from the winter rains, and after the church a few cottages, and then the little town that was called El Rocio, because of the "dew" that covered the *marismas* every morning. She'd remained there ever since.

For fifty-one weeks of the year Rocio itself was a ghost town, with barely a dozen families living in the white-walled enclave. Then two or three days before Whitsunday and depending on the distance they had to travel, the forty-four brotherhoods—which had grown up in honour of the Blanca Paloma, the White Dove, as the Virgin was known—would set out from towns and villages across Andalucía, and ride into the marshes to pay her homage. They'd meet in Rocio on Sunday, kneel in the streets next morning as she was carried through the town by the men of Almonte who'd found her first, and then separate to ride back through the marshes to the towns where they'd started.

During that one week alone the entire *marismas* belonged to the Rocieros, the pilgrims of the Rocio. Not even the Coto, with all its guards and fences, was sacrosanct. The mounted squadrons of the brotherhoods from the south, with the cavalcade of carts and mules and caravans which followed them like the baggage train of an army, would ride through it twice; once on the way to Rocio, once on the way back. And both times they'd camp at night on the stretch of plain round the *palacio*.

Carswell folded the newspaper, put it aside and lay back on his pillow. The pilgrimage of the Rocio wasn't only the answer to the first of his problems; by chance it had suggested a solution to the second—how to draw Samir away from his guards. The emblem of the pilgrimage, printed at the head of each of the pages in the supplement, was the silhouette of a wild bird.

The bird was a dove. Yet with its wings curved back in flight, it looked identical to the harrier that had struck at the partridge and thrown off Samir's falcon.

For the ten minutes which followed the harrier's attack, Samir had ridden alone half a mile in front of his companions.

'Hey, Minette—'

Carswell tugged at her ear-lobe. It was two o'clock and the room was hazy with the afternoon heat.

'If you sleep any more you'll grow fat!'

She stretched drowsily.

'I'm hungry.'

He laughed. 'We'll eat. Then I've got a hell of a lot to do. How would you like to go to a party? Not the usual sort of party. For one thing, most of it's on horseback, and then it goes on for five days and nights.'

'You kidding me, Carswell?'

'I'm not kidding you—'

He told her about the pilgrimage to Rocio.

'But how do we do it?' she said as he finished. 'You've got nothing to ride on, and anyway I've never been near a fucking horse in my life—'

'I'll walk, lots of the pilgrims do that, and I'll see if I can hire a mule to carry you and the other things.'

'A mule?'

Carswell laughed at the expression of terror on her face.

'Like a horse,' he said. 'Only slower and more comfortable. That's if I can find one which behaves.'

'And then what? All right, so we get to this place with all the people. But how's that going to help? If they're so worried about this man, they probably won't let him out; maybe they'll even move him somewhere else while it's happening.'

He shook his head. Carswell had considered the possibility before he went to sleep.

The *palacio* itself wouldn't be affected by the riders, only the grounds round it. Outside, it was true, the security problems would be appalling, but only in the immediate area; the rest of the Coto, away from the route to Rocio, would still be deserted. He also doubted whether Samir would agree even if they wanted him to move. The London brief had described him as wilful and obstinate; if the hawking had been one of the main reasons which had brought him there in the first place, he'd be unlikely to miss a week at the height of the season.

More likely they'd double the guards round the building, which Carswell had already abandoned as impregnable, and use one of the Land-Rovers to take him well clear of the Rocio concourse every morning before allowing him to mount.

'They'll change the pattern of course,' he said, 'but I believe we'll still find him there and he'll still be going out every day.'

'Even if he is, what about all those other people with him, the ones you told me about? They'll stay even closer now.'

Carswell nodded. 'Unless something happens to take him away from them for a while. All I need is five or ten minutes. And I think I can make something happen which'll give me that time.'

After lunch, Carswell got ready to leave again.

'I'm afraid I'll be away all night again,' he said. 'But I'll be back by ten tomorrow morning—'

'Bad lay?'

Minette burst into laughter as he frowned at her.

'A fellow who picks up a girl, spends one night with her, then skips out all the rest, Christ, it's not very flattering, is it?'

He laughed too. 'I'll make up for it afterwards.'

'Afterwards?' She stopped laughing instantly. 'What's going to happen afterwards, Carswell?'

'Let's just get this over with first—'

'Please come back soon.'

She cut him off abruptly, rolled onto her side in bed and lay with her face turned towards the wall.

* * *

Two hours later he drove into Sanlúcar de Barrameda, a dirty sun-baked, low-lying town where the Guadalquivir estuary ran into the sea.

The hotel manager's cousin had an old Seat van which he used to collect eggs from his farm outside the town every Monday. The rest of the week it was parked behind the hotel. Carswell had noticed him unloading it that morning and arranged to hire it for the next twenty-four hours.

Sanlúcar was only twenty miles beyond the little village of Benalmartín, where he'd alighted from the bus two days earlier and walked through the fields to the river bank from which he'd swum across to the Coto. The estuary was broader here but he could see the shore of the preserve as he came out onto the harbour front, a low line of sand and trees shimmering distantly across the water.

Carswell found a crowded café and went up to the bar. He'd chosen Sanlúcar because it was from there that three of the largest and oldest brotherhoods, those of Cádiz, Jerez and Sanlúcar itself, set out on the journey to Rocio, crossing the estuary in ancient cattle ferries before riding for two days across the entire length of the Coto until they reached the Virgin's sanctuary just beyond the northern boundary.

By seven, as dusk was falling and after being sent from stable to blacksmith's forge and then back again to innumerable other stables, he'd got what he wanted; a mule for the length of the pilgrimage, a hut in which to stable it until they left, two cavernous wicker side-panniers and a number of other purchases he'd made in a chandler's behind the harbour.

When he'd left the hotel he'd taken LeKahn's gun-case. He removed it from the van, put it on one of the roof-beams that ran across the top of the hut and padlocked the rickety door; it was unlikely anyone would try to break in but if they did they'd almost certainly miss the squat leather box on the cob-webbed ledge overhead. Then he drove out of Sanlúcar, along the main road back towards Sevilla, and halfway there turned right into the sierras.

It was a further hour before he saw what he was looking for. By then the sun had set and the air was darkening. He rounded a corner, saw a glittering expanse of water and beyond it a single rocky crag rearing up above the lake like an immense solitary watch-tower. The battlements of the fortress at its peak were silhouetted against the evening sky, and the last of the light flared off a huddle of white cottages beneath.

He drove round the lake and parked the van at the base of the hill. The fortress was a thousand feet above him. For a time there was nothing except the great shelf of tumbled rocks, the crumbling ruin of the keep and the pale bowl of the sky. Then something seemed to fall from thousands of feet higher still, a tiny stone-coloured object that plunged down until it almost struck the battlements. At the last moment, it curled sideways, a pair of barred wings beat at the air, it soared briefly again and finally planed down to vanish in one of the holes in the masonry.

Carswell smiled to himself, walked forward and began to climb. A few yards above the road he passed the blue-and-white lettered sign, CASTELLAR DE LA FRONTERA.

It was ten years since he'd visited Castellar, but his memory was right: the birds had been there then, they were still there now—just as they'd been for five hundred years. Castellar. One of the last outposts of the Moorish kingdom in Spain. A lonely defiant strong-point that had held firm against the armies of the Catholic monarchs, advancing to reconquer the country from the north, for half a century after the rest of Andalucía had been won back.

Defiant—but finally subdued. The Spanish force had fought its way up the same shelf of rock he was climbing now, they'd slaughtered the Moorish garrison inside the fortress and then, to signal the victory to the surrounding countryside, they'd set fire to Castellar—turning castle and village into one huge beacon of flame. Every living creature there had died—except the hawks.

Set free when the fire burnt through the wooden trellises of the mews cages, they took to the air. For a week they circled the burning fortress. Then, as the flames died down, they returned to nest in the gapped and damaged walls. They'd been there ever since, kestrels, goshawks, merlins, falcons, the largest colony of predators in Europe.

It was the printed emblem of the dove in the newspaper, so much like a marsh harrier, which had reminded Carswell. Samir's behaviour after the wild hawk stooped had been, in retrospect, predictable. Caught up in the excitement of the chase and fiercely proud of his own skill, he'd waved the others back—so they wouldn't further unsettle his own falcon circling overhead—and had ridden forward until he'd flighted the partridge again.

When the hawk stooped for the second time Samir had been half a mile from the horsemen and further still from the Land-Rovers. If the incident had happened in the dunes rather than the plain, he'd have been out of sight of them all.

Providing he could capture a couple of the wild hawks of Castellar and release them at the right moment in the Coto, there was a possibility Carswell could create the situation again—and this time beyond the view of anyone except Samir.

He reached the base of the castle's containing wall, worked his way round until he came to the main archway and walked into the keep. The whole fortress was silent and deserted; the few villagers who'd lived in the cottages outside had moved away years before and only the occasional shepherd used it now to shelter his flock in winter. Looking round in the light of the moon, Carswell noticed a shadowed alcove. He dimly remembered that a staircase inside led up to the roof. He pushed aside a rotted door and began to climb.

At the top of the stairs he came out onto a balustraded terrace. The air had been close in the courtyard below. Now, two thousand feet above sea-level, it was fresh and clear and cool. A light wind whistled in the arrow slits of the walls and an owl floated away from its perch on a stone water-funnel. He walked over to the parapet, leaned forward, lowered his head and listened; below the fluting wind and the owl calls he could hear something else—the rustle and stir of feathers in a fissure below.

He went back to the centre of the roof, unpacked a length of knotted rope from the canvas satchel containing his purchases at the Sanlúcar chandlers, and knotted one end round a stone pillar by the doorway. He paid out the rope until he reached the parapet again, wound it twice round his right leg and chest, swung himself onto the ledge and cautiously began to lower himself down the far side.

For a moment all went well. Then, as he reached the top of the keep's outer wall, there was a sudden jolt and the rope slipped as if it had been cut. Carswell felt himself plunge down, a second jolt which tore at his ankle and a burning pain on his leg. Somehow, just as he thought the rope had run out altogether and he'd fall the thousand feet to the rocks below, he managed to get both hands above his head, lock them round the last of the knots and hold himself there, ten feet below the parapet.

He discovered what had happened half an hour later when he regained the parapet. In the darkness he hadn't noticed that the rain had carved a deep groove in the balustrade at the point where he'd climbed over. The rope had slipped into the groove, dropped to the bottom and the twelve inches of free-fall had almost dislodged him. At the time all he could do was hang there, sweating and panting, with the stones butting against his ribs, until he'd recovered. Then he began to heave himself back towards the top.

It took him five minutes to reach the level of the fissure where he'd heard the rustle of feathers. He wedged one foot in a crack, coiled the rope tighter round his arm and fumbled in the satchel for a torch. He pulled it out and flashed it quickly into the blackness. There was a vicious hiss, wings stiffened against the stone and a pair of brilliant yellow eyes shone for an instant above a curved beak.

Carswell put the torch away, drew out a baggy purse net and spread it over the mouth of the hole, hooking the cord rim onto angles of the stonework. Then he hauled himself up to the parapet, regained his breath and rummaged in the satchel again. He found a length of plastic tubing which he bent into a rough L shape, and lowered the tube over the wall until its arm was sticking through the net into the fissure. He sucked hard on a small black cigar and puffed the smoke down the tube. Wisps of greyness seeped out of the hole.

He'd smoked almost half the cigar before the bird decided it couldn't take the fumes any longer. There was a sudden stir, the scrape of talons on rock, then a heavy tug at the cord which he'd looped round his wrist. Carswell pulled up the net and held it swinging in front of him. The bird, a full-grown male peregrine, was lying trapped inside; its wings, enmeshed in the netting, were shaking and the horn scimitar of its beak slashed furiously at the string.

He laid the bundle down, put on a pair of leather gloves and took the last of his purchases from the satchel—some fishermen's woolen socks from which he'd sliced off the feet. He waited until the hawk had momentarily exhausted itself. Then he grasped its back with one hand and worked the woolen sleeve over its head with the other. Afterwards he disentangled it from the net and dropped it, still quivering but totally imprisoned now, into the satchel.

Finally he sat down and lit a cigarette. The whole operation had taken him more than an hour; he'd lost most of the skin on his right palm, there was a long burn mark running round his leg from ankle to thigh, his ribs were bruised from the jagged points of the stonework and his fore-arm was bleeding from a cluster of cuts where the bird's talons had caught him as he encased it in the sock. But he'd got what he was after—or one of them at least. He'd decided he'd need two wild hawks; to be safe, in case anything happened to either of them, he should have a third.

He ground out his cigarette, coiled the rope round himself and started again.

It was four o'clock when he finished. By then, in addition to the male peregrine, the satchel contained a merlin and a female peregrine—identical to the bird which Samir had flown at the partridge. All three were lying blind and helpless in lengths of the thick wool. Carswell slung the bag over his shoulder, the satchel twelve pounds heavier now than when he'd started, and set off down towards the van.

The sun was already high and day's heat was gathering when he walked upstairs to the hotel bedroom. He'd driven first to Sanlúcar, left the hawks still imprisoned in the woolen sleeves on the floor of the stable where the mule was chewing methodically through a bale of straw, and returned to Sevilla.

The pilgrimage to Rocio would start at dawn the following morning. If his plan worked, the Robespierre serial was only a few days from its conclusion.

16

London

'What's his mood this morning?'

'A combination of barely controlled frenzy and terminal shock,' Cazenove said. 'When he learns about this—'

He stabbed at the photograph on Handley-Reid's desk.

'He'll go straight off the edge. He initialled every one of the annual estimates without looking at a single figure. I could have put the Treaty of Versailles in front of him, and he'd have signed it without a second thought. Only now—'

He shook his head and whistled. Handley-Reid picked up the photograph and studied it again.

It was Friday, the day before the Director's deadline for finding Carswell expired. The meeting on the Robespierre serial was due to start in a few minutes.

When he'd arrived that morning Handley-Reid still hadn't decided how to present his report. In the week since the Director had instructed them to trace and stop Carswell, they'd achieved nothing. The Spanish resident had been in constant contact with the Madrid criminal investigation bureau; he'd given them Carswell's file photograph, together with an elaborate explanation; and a major police search had been launched in the south.

The results had been negative. There hadn't even been a report of a single sighting which could plausibly be attached to either Carswell or the girl. They had both simply disappeared.

As the week passed Handley-Reid felt increasingly optimistic.

Even if the war rules hypothesis was correct, that Carswell had learned Samir's hiding-place from the girl and set out to complete the serial, it seemed inconceivable he'd evaded both the massive hunt in the Guadalajara mountains and also the search which had been initiated five hundred miles further south.

More likely he'd gone to ground—unable to break through the police cordon. The last Madrid Telex, repeating the message of the past six days—that nothing had emerged from the two continuing investigations—appeared to confirm that.

Handley-Reid had read the Telex at ten. Fifteen minutes afterwards, as he was choosing the phrases in which to tell the Director it now looked as if the Carswell threat could be discounted, a call had come through from Grosvenor Square. The American embassy's department of European Studies (as the CIA London bureau called itself) had just received a certain document from Paris: would a member of Handley-Reid's staff call round urgently to collect it?

He despatched Spencer immediately. Spencer returned an hour later with a large envelope. The "document" inside was a photograph, not of Carswell—but of the girl. The print was a blow-up of a police criminal records picture. It showed her head and shoulders with her face staring directly at the camera; a number had been stencilled in red ink on the border and the name, Marie Vercors, written below.

'Sulky little thing, isn't she?' Cazenove peered over Handley-Reid's shoulder. 'What the Christ can Carswell be doing with her?'

'First, we don't know he is with her,' Handley-Reid said. 'Secondly, they're far from sure she's the same one this GI poked. That's it, isn't it, Spencer?'

Spencer straightened up on the other side of the room.

'Yes, sir. Apparently the man spent a couple of hours with her. He picked her up in a café; he can't remember where but he thinks it was somewhere near the station. They had something to eat. Then he drove out into the country and—'

'For Christ's sake,' Handley-Reid snapped, 'he banged her, didn't he?'

Spencer flushed.

'That's what they told me, sir. Afterwards, he drove back into the city, paid her and dropped her near the station again. He's certain she was French—she couldn't speak much English and he recognized her accent—but he also said she was a blonde.'

'Dyed her hair?'

'They suggested that, sir.' Spencer nodded. 'It's all very vague because I gather there are any number of foreign prostitutes in the towns near the American bases out there. Also, the man had been drinking heavily. But they seem to be taking it quite seriously.'

Cazenove gave a short rasping laugh.

'If it is the same girl, Charles,' he said, 'and if she is with Carswell, then we seem not only to have landed up with an agent running out of control—we've got one who's gone in for pimping too!'

The idea had obviously originated with Vavasseur. The thinking behind it, the psychological assessment and the calculations, was characteristic of him. Handley-Reid realized that as soon as Spencer got back from the embassy.

Vavasseur had worked through the French Sûreté, probably using the Agency's relationship with SDECE to make sure they co-operated without an explanation. The earlier SDECE signals had shown LeKahn was already on file and under movement surveillance. It had probably taken the Sûreté office in Marseilles only a few hours to learn the girl's identity, establish that she had a criminal record and come up with the photograph Vavasseur wanted.

The photograph had been copied and given a mass distribution throughout the American bases in southern Spain—with the instruction for any serviceman recognizing the girl to report immediately to his base commander. A young French girl, on the run from the police, presumably short of money and a whore by profession—it was logical she'd head towards a town where she could earn enough to get back to her own country. She must have guessed the land border between France and Spain would be sealed after the two killings; it left her with no option but to head south.

That at least must have been Vavasseur's guess. If the GI was right, it was precisely what she'd done. From Vavasseur's point of view the girl herself was unimportant. Her sole interest lay in being able to tell him whether there'd been someone else with the Belgian. That in turn depended on finding her.

For Handley-Reid the implications were quite different. He couldn't think of any reason why Carswell should have taken the girl with him. But if he had done (and it was difficult to imagine how she could have slipped through the police cordon without Carswell's help), and if she was in Sevilla, then the Director's acid summary of the situation at last week's meeting had been correct.

Three days before the Cairo conference started, they had one of their agents within a hundred miles of the Robespierre serial's subject—and one who was presumably making his final preparations to assassinate Samir.

'The treacherous little sod!' Handley-Reid's anger towards the Arab flared again. 'Well, we'd better be going downstairs, hadn't we?'

He turned to Cazenove. 'Are we going to have the pleasure of your company, Peter?'

'Doubt if I've got any option.' Cazenove shrugged. 'Don't get me wrong, Charles, I'm right with you however our prima ballerina responds. But what the hell are you going to tell him?'

'The whole bloody story.'

Handley-Reid curtly indicated to Spencer that he pick up the photograph.

'He sanctioned the serial from the start. Now he wants this man stopped. Fine. He can just see it through to the finish.'

'Meaning what?'

'Meaning I'm not going to let that little bastard get away with it. He's screwed us all the way down the line from Riyadh to Geneva to the games he was playing with Vavasseur. He can even screw us now, although he won't have the satisfaction of knowing it; if this, what's he called—?'

'Carswell.'

'Carswell—gets to him, he'll still have screwed us. And that's something he's not going to do.'

Cazenove frowned. 'But there's damn all more—'

'There is.' Handley-Reid nodded. 'Isn't one of Gerry Fenton's sidelines liaison with Special Branch?'

'That's right. He handles protection groups for VIP overseas tours. Why?'

'Because we happen to have a VIP overseas. Not one of our own this time, but sure as hell a VIP. So Gerry's going to send a unit of SB marksmen out there to join Vavasseur's people. A dozen of them, the best SB's got, fully briefed, with Carswell's photograph, his description, the lot. Vavasseur can't object; we've got access now and we're just doubling the guard in our own interests—"unspecified threats" or something. Christ knows, we were "right" the first time.'

There was silence for a moment. Then Cazenove whistled and gestured in the direction of the Director's office.

'Is he going to stand for it?'

'*Stand* for it?' Handley-Reid smiled. 'He's got no bloody choice. What did he say himself? If they ever even learn about the serial, they'll start to think Philby was a missing coffee-break memo. And that was when we didn't intend to kill the little sod. So what the hell can he do now when it could actually happen?'

17

Sevilla

'Minette—'

'What is it?' She shook her hair loose on the pillow and looked up drowsily. 'What is it?'

'Where did you get these?'

Carswell had found them in a drawer below the cupboard a moment earlier when he'd been looking for the key to Le-Kahn's gun-case: three green one-thousand-peseta notes.

They hadn't been there four days before when he'd hidden the key after dismantling the Mannlicher. Now he held them up in front of her. The afternoon was hot and the cathedral clock was chiming across the roofs beyond the window.

'What the fuck's that got to do with you?'

She saw the notes, sat up and glared at him.

'I want to know—'

'They're mine.'

'Where did you get them?'

'*Fiches moi la paix!* I don't go prying through your things, you just leave mine alone too.'

It was the first time in a week he'd seen her angry. Carswell lowered his hand but went on watching her expressionlessly—waiting. After a moment she shrugged and looked away.

'You've gone and spoilt everything, Carswell.' Her voice was petulant. 'That was my surprise for you if we ran out of money. Jean gave them to me. I had them all the time and I never told you—'

'You didn't have anything, Jean didn't give you anything,' Carswell said. 'You went out last night while I was away and you picked up someone and you hustled them. That's what happened, wasn't it?'

'What if it was—?'

She yawned, closed her eyes and rolled over to face the wall. 'I wasn't going to cheat you, I'd have given them to you anyway.'

'For Christ's sake, Minette!' He reached forward and caught her wrist. 'I'm not your bloody Corsican, I don't care what you were going to do with the money. I just want to know how you got it. Was it last night? Or the one before?'

'That one, when you went away the first time—'

She told him. She'd been bored and had gone out to the café across the street, where Carswell had told her to wait for an hour if he was ever late in returning.

Minette had meant to have a coffee and watch the evening *paseo*. An American, a master sergeant from the base at Rota, had joined her at the table almost as soon as she'd sat down. They'd talked for a while, he'd insisted she have dinner with him, then they'd driven out into the country in his car.

'But I was going to give you the money—'

'Where did he leave you?'

'I made him stop up the other end of the street. Christ, I'm not that stupid—I wasn't going to let him know where I lived.'

Minette wriggled round frowning.

'Come on, Carswell, I only got us some money, didn't I? What are you so screwed up about?'

'Listen,' he said. 'For all we know the whole Spanish police force is still looking for us—for you anyway. They know you're French and they'll have a good description, even if your hair's a different colour now—'

Carswell had just showered when he'd found the notes and he had a towel knotted round his waist. He got off the bed and began to dress.

'What the hell do you think's going to happen if they put out that description to the military police at the American bases? It's possible; they've done it before when there've been crimes involving foreigners—let alone a double killing. And suppose this master sergeant of yours remembered yesterday when he sobered up, what's going to happen then?'

She gazed across the room at him, wide-eyed, penitent, the sheets drawn up round her chin so that only the upper half of her face showed against the shadowed bed-stead.

'You're a stupid thoughtless little fool—'

He broke off, shook his head and laughed.

It was impossible. In his first immediate worry about the danger she might have created for them both, Carswell hadn't even considered his own response. Now he found he couldn't even feel anger, let alone jealousy or resentment. Somehow she created her own rules, demanded that she be accepted as she was without qualification; earthy, unsentimental, seeing things clearly and simply in the way she'd taught herself to look at them, living from situation to situation without regret or false hope, making in each of them pockets of pleasure, delight, laughter—above all, laughter.

'God damn you, Minette!'

As he laughed again she leapt out of bed, ran naked across the floor and threw her arms round his neck.

'I knew you were all right really, Carswell. And next time I truly will give them to you—'

'Next time? First of all, there's not going to be a next time—not while I'm around anyway. And then I thought these *were* for me, weren't they?'

'Course, they were. Only—' She paused.

'Let's have it.'

'Well, I was looking in that book.' She pointed at the pamphlet on the Coto. 'It's got pictures of this thing we're going on, you know with all the horses and people and that. And the women, they're all wearing those long dresses—'

'So you want to buy yourself a flamenco dress, is that it?'

'Not really, Carswell.' She looked at him tentatively. 'I mean, if you really need the money—'

'God Almighty, you're incorrigible, Minette! Go away and get dressed.'

He disentangled himself.

'All right, you can have your dress. We'll get that later this evening. Meanwhile, there are some other things I want to buy for tomorrow. I'll be back by seven. And Christ help you if I discover you've "found" any more money while I'm out!'

Carswell noticed the man at the end of the street.

He came through the archway of the *guardia civil* building at the intersection as Carswell reached it; young, dark-suited, alert-faced, probably a clerk in an administration section. Later Carswell remembered that he'd seemed to hesitate as he passed. At the time he simply walked on, crossed the road and went into a tobacconist.

Carswell saw him again when he came out, standing on the far pavement. As soon as Carswell appeared he glanced round as if he was looking for a cab. Carswell turned right and walked casually in the opposite direction. Five minutes later he knew it wasn't a coincidence: the man was following him.

Carswell had turned into an alleyway and stopped at a newspaper kiosk twenty yards down from the street. Pretending to search for a paper in the wire racks, he watched the plastic canopy above the kiosk. He saw the man appear behind him, pause while he glanced down the alleyway and then, when he'd seen Carswell's back, busy himself examining a row of pewter jugs hanging outside a shop at the corner.

The incident was baffling and disturbing. Carswell was certain he'd never seen the man before and equally certain that their encounter outside the *guardia civil* building had happened completely by chance. Even if the Guadalajara police hunt had spread to the south, his own description would have been far too vague and commonplace for the man to identify him—least of all in the few seconds when he must have glimpsed Carswell's face.

Whatever the explanation it was imperative he lose the man, get back to the hotel and move out immediately, so that they were away from the city. The Rocio pilgrimage started the next day. He'd planned to rise at dawn, take the bus down to Sanlúcar and cross into the *marismas* with the first of the southern brotherhoods, when they boarded the ferries at eight. Now he'd have to find somewhere else to spend the night.

Carswell chose a paper and pushed it across the counter. In front of him, towering against the darkening sky, he could see the spire of the cathedral. Beyond it was the great open square of the Reyes Católicas with the Barrio de Santa Cruz on the far side—a warren of narrow winding streets and alleys, walled with the great mansions of the Sevillana gentry and interspersed with tiny squares, courtyards, fountains and gardens.

His best chance of losing the man was inside the Barrio. Carswell pocketed his change and set off towards the cathedral. In the square on the far side he casually dropped his paper, bent down to pick it up and glanced back. The man had just come out of the *mesquita* gateway behind him, a dark silhouette against the lowering sun. He moved and Carswell lost him in the wall's shadow.

When Carswell saw him again the man was talking to a pair of patrolling *guardia civil*. By then Carswell had reached the centre of the square, with the entrance to the Barrio fifty yards ahead. He stopped by a tiled seat, lifted his foot as if he was tying a shoe-lace and looked back again. As he watched, the man raised his arm, pointed at Carswell and all three of them started to walk towards him.

Carswell straightened up and, walking faster now, headed for the arch that led into the Barrio. Behind him there was a shout and the sound of running feet. The arch was only ten yards away now but the intervening space was brilliant with golden dusty light. Carswell could see his shadow stretching out, black and knife-edged on the worn flagstones. Suddenly, with his own silhouette cutting across the walls in front, he felt utterly naked and vulnerable.

He raced forward, ducked under the arch, swung round the buttress of a carriage yard and ran down a cobbled alley. The sunlight had been sliced off abruptly by the Barrio's outer wall and the alley was in half-darkness. He'd almost reached the far end when the shot was fired. The bullet ricochetted off the stonework above his head, scattering fragments of brick and plaster on the cobbles. In the enclosed windless space between the houses the sound was deafening. Carswell dived into a doorway, dropped to his knees and peered back; he was panting and sweating and his legs shook.

There were three silhouettes now, all of them black against the keyhole of light where the alley emerged into the square. Two were upright; the third was half crouching, his legs splayed apart and his arm held stiffly forward in front of his face. Carswell waited, motionless. They walked forwards, slowly at first, then faster when nothing happened, until they were all running again.

When they were thirty feet away, he stood up, stepped into the slender line of sunlight at the street's centre, forced himself to stand there frozen for a moment, then plunged into another doorway on the far side. As he'd guessed, they stopped instantly. The leading policeman knelt down and fired again as Carswell threw himself back into the shadow, the bullet lower this time and shattering a ground-floor window. As the gun-bolt clicked for a third shot and the echoes of the falling glass were still reverberating against the walls, Carswell launched himself at the end of the street, swayed round another buttress and ran zig-zagging up the alley beyond.

Ten minutes afterwards he was out of the Barrio and back in the busy streets of the town centre. The man from the *guardia civil* post and the two policemen were presumably still hunting for him inside the Barrio. It was impossible for him to go back to the hotel. As soon as a general alert went out, the area round the station where he'd been spotted first would be the focus of the search. All he could do was head for the bus terminal outside the city and hope that Minette followed the fail-safe routine he'd been over with her so many times since they'd arrived.

Carswell hailed a taxi and settled back in his seat. They'd almost reached the terminal when he suddenly remembered that the *guardia civil* were only empowered to fire if they came under attack themselves, or if they were in pursuit of a known criminal.

The young man in the dark suit hadn't merely been suspicious of Carswell—he'd been certain of his identity. He couldn't have known that on the basis of a vague verbal description. He'd have needed something else, something specific and unmistakeable, something that Carswell could only guess was a photograph.

Minette joined him at ten o'clock. By then Carswell had almost given up hope; the terminal was only twenty minutes by taxi from the hotel, and if she'd followed his instructions she should have arrived by nine at the latest.

He ordered a final cognac in the café beside the rows of buses and decided that if she wasn't there by the time he'd drunk it, he'd have to leave for Sanlúcar on his own. He was just finishing when he saw her on the street outside, taller than the surrounding Spaniards, her shirt pale against her brown arms and her face frowning as she searched the crowd.

'Minette, thank Christ!'

Carswell pushed his way through the tables and put his arm round her shoulder.

'Carswell.' She leant against him. 'Was I right? I just didn't know—'

'You were utterly right. Here—'

He led her inside, sat her down at the table and called for another cognac.

'What happened?' She looked at him, worried. 'I wasn't even thinking, really. I washed my hair and I was just sort of messing around. Then I suddenly noticed the clock. You said seven and it was half past. So I went straight to the café and you still didn't come. Then I couldn't get a taxi. Christ, it was fucking ages—'

'But you found one?'

She nodded. 'He even spoke some English, well, my sort of English. I asked him about buses to Córdoba, just like you said. I think I talked too much, because he wanted to stay and take me out to dinner.'

Carswell laughed and put his arms round her again. For an instant nothing mattered except that she'd arrived, that she was still with him.

'But what happened?' she repeated. 'Why didn't you come back?'

He told her about the man who'd followed him, the chase through the Barrio and the shots being fired. When he'd finished she grasped his wrist anxiously.

'Because of me, Carswell, because of that American?'

Carswell shook his head. 'No, Minette. It was something else.'

Two hours later he was no closer to understanding. The man's identification of him had been positive and immediate—the shots proved that. The more Carswell thought about it, the more certain he became it could only have happened through a photograph. A photograph that had been intensively circulated to the Sevilla police. If that was so, the man must have studied it, memorized Carswell's features and then, quite accidentally, fitted them to him in the chance meeting on the street.

Yet he was still bewildered how they could have got a photograph in the first place. The only possible explanation was that it came from the Americans. Perhaps he'd been noticed after all, as he followed LeKahn. If the Belgian's trail had been picked up earlier than he'd guessed, they might also have seen and photographed Carswell—using one of the long-range telephoto cameras that had become standard surveillance equipment.

At the time it could have been merely a precautionary measure. But when the posada manager was killed, the girl vanished and Carswell disappeared too, they could have decided he was the Belgian's stand-by. Then, having lost him themselves, they might have co-opted the assistance of the Spanish police—feeding them the photograph with some cover story to avoid implicating themselves in LeKahn's murder.

For the moment any explanation was irrelevant. Only one fact mattered: the Spanish police knew his identity, had discovered he was in the area and would intensify their hunt for him.

They alighted in Sanlúcar's main square at one o'clock. Carswell collected the mule from the little stable on the outskirts of the town. He settled the panniers on its back with the guncase, the provisions he'd bought for the journey and the three hawks, still encased in the woolen stockings, packed inside. The mule was docile and somnolent, but the three birds vibrated with impotent fury when he transferred them to the panniers. Then he walked down to the waterfront.

He found the hulk of an old beached fishing-boat and tied the mule's halter to its rotting rudder-stem.

'Tonight's hotel,' he said.

Minette glanced down at the sand. 'Jesus, right here?'

Carswell nodded. 'Think you'll be able to sleep?'

She laughed. 'Hang about with you much longer and I'll be sleeping by my ankles from a church steeple. This is easy—like old times!'

She scooped out a trough in the sand and lay down on her side as she'd done in the mountains.

For a while Carswell lay beside her. Many horses had crossed the estuary that evening before the ferries stopped, but there were still hundreds of them tethered to the rails in front of the bars and warehouses that bordered the shore. Carswell could hear them in the darkness; the quiet stamp of hoofs, the rustle of a shaken mane, the clink of an iron stirrup against the wooden poles. Finally, unable to sleep, he stood up and strolled along the beach.

The sand was covered with sleeping bodies, mostly gypsies who'd trekked from miles back in the sierras for the pilgrimage. Carts, wagons and caravans, waiting for the ferries to start again at first light, pressed down to the edge of the water. He passed a driftwood fire with an old man huddled into a cape nodding slowly to himself, a litter of children lying tumbled across each other, an entire family covered by a single sheepskin rug—on every side the shuffles, grunts and stirrings of a huge crowd asleep.

Then he reached a ferry-point, walked out along the ramshackle wooden platform and looked at the far shore. Behind him the night sounds of the concourse were interwoven with the stench of sour wine and dried sweat, horse droppings and axle-oil, saltwater and mud. In front he could see the faint white line of the sand with a darker bar above, the trees and scrub that rimmed the Coto, and at the centre the glow of a lamp on the landing-stage.

Thirty miles to the north Samir would be asleep in some upper room of the *palacio*. Samir. That—not the sounds and smells of the Rocio pilgrims on the beach—was the reason Carswell couldn't sleep. The little Arab with the feral face and the pale shifting almond eyes.

It wasn't so much the thought of killing him which had kept Carswell awake. Something else, some incongruity between the way he'd imagined the Arab from the London file and the way the man had actually looked. "Devious, arrogant, deceitful and totally unpredictable in his behavioural patterns"—those were just a few of the phrases London had used to describe him.

The Samir he'd watched didn't match that characterization

at all. Instead, the Arab had been confident, direct, assured of his mastery of horse and falcon, sunlit and brilliant in the white robe, golden head-cord and jewelled belt, laughing and—happy. That was what Carswell hadn't expected, where the two images collided.

Whoever had written the file had seen Samir in a different context; frightened, threatened, perhaps even desperate. Carswell had seen him in a world that the man understood and loved. And that had changed everything.

Everything—except Carswell knew he wouldn't have been aware of the contradiction between the two images if something hadn't changed in him too, something that allowed him to see not furtiveness and deceit but laughter.

His cigarette hissed as he flicked it into the water. Minette. Her hand raking down his face. The implacable defiance in her voice and the calculated viciousness when she'd attacked him with the broken bottle. The contours of her body sprawled over his. The pride in the more than "two hundred" men she'd had. The notes hidden in the drawer. The naïveté, the absolute confidence, the changes of allegiance as casual as the change of a blouse, the delight in a meal at a cheap restaurant as total as if she'd suddenly discovered she'd inherited a million francs, the laughter.

That was the link. Between Samir, between her, between himself. That was what the London brief had missed. That was what he'd learned, where the change had come. Carswell walked back to the beached hulk and lay down beside Minette again. This time he didn't think about anything.

Instead, resolutely, deliberately, unwaveringly he concentrated on the passage of the constellations above the black curve of the boat's gunwale. Eventually he slept.

'Carswell!'

Minette was shaking him urgently. He jerked up and looked round. The light was grey with dawn and everywhere on the beach people were packing up the night's camp and getting ready to embark. Both the ferries were half-loaded and long lines of wagons, mules, horses and donkeys had formed at each of the jetties.

'Look!' She pointed across the sand. *'Flics!'*

Peering in the direction of her arm under the hull of the boat he saw a dozen *guardias*. They'd obviously just arrived and a captain was giving them orders. As Carswell watched they separated into couples, one pair going to each of the ferries and the others spreading out to patrol the approaches to the shore.

'Are they looking for us?'

'They're certainly after me—'

Carswell glanced round. A few yards away was a family of gypsies—half a dozen children, two women and an ancient canvas-covered cart. The man had greeted him the previous night and offered him a drink.

'Wait here a moment.'

The patrolling *guardias* were still on the far side of the boat, hidden from them by the hull. Carswell stood up, walked over to the cart where the gypsy was tightening the axlebolt and knelt down.

'Muy buenas.'

The gypsy looked up and grinned. *'Ola, hombre, que tal?'*

'Oye—'

Carswell gave him a cigarette, jerked his thumb back towards Minette and explained she wasn't well, the woman's trouble. The gypsy's wife, who'd come round to listen, nodded sympathetically. Would they let her ride over in the cart? She was bad on the water anyway and the trouble made it worse. If she could just lie down for a while, cross in comfort and then rest on the other side, she'd be all right for the journey.

The gypsy clapped his arm round Carswell's shoulder laughing.

'*Hombre, que va? Es el Rocio, no? Mujer*—'

He turned to his wife, but she'd already gone over to the boat. Carswell thanked him and went back to Minette and the gypsy's wife.

'Listen.' Carswell put his arm protectively round Minette's waist. 'You've got the curse badly—so look ill. These people are going to take you over in their cart. I don't think the police are looking for you, but if you lie down in the back you'll be fine.'

'What about you?'

'I'll work something out. Don't worry, I'll join you over there as soon as I can.'

Minette looked at him anxiously for a moment. Then she turned back to the woman and allowed herself to be led over to the cart. Carswell watched her climb in and disappear under its canvas hood.

He lowered himself under the keel of the boat again. A pair of *guardias* was standing on the beach by each of the jetties, checking the pilgrims as they boarded the ferries. With the ramps of the boats in the water and in the general confused struggle to manhandle heavy carriages on board or force frightened and recalcitrant horses, mules and donkeys through the waves, they were able to give each passenger only a cursory glance.

Carswell glanced back at where the gypsy's cart had been parked behind him. It had disappeared now and a few minutes later he spotted it being trundled into line at another ferry-point to his right. The gypsy was leading the mule and Carswell could see the silhouette of the man's wife on the driving bench. There was no sign of Minette.

He waited until the cart rumbled into the open hold. Then he turned to watch the other jetty.

The chance came half an hour later. A heavy barrel-laden wagon, probably a wine cart for one of the brotherhoods, passed within a few feet of the boat's hull. It was being pulled by five mules and the two drivers were having difficulty in controlling the animals.

As it went by, one of the mules shied and reared, dragging the wagon sideways so that the wheels dug into the damp churned-up sand at the water's edge. One of the men lashed at the plunging animal while the other ran to the back, put his shoulder against the tail-board and tried to heave the rear wheels away from the sea.

Carswell glanced under the keel. The patrolling teams of *guardias* were fifty yards from the boat, with their backs to him. He stood up and sprinted over to the wagon.

'*Les ayudo?*'

The man, straining against the tail-board, smiled gratefully.

'*Y la mula?*'

Carswell gestured at the panniered mule, still tethered to the boat's rudder, and the man indicated an iron bar above the wheels.

Carswell ran back to the boat, unhitched the mule, pulled it behind him to the wagon and tied its halter round the bar.

As soon as he'd helped push the wagon back onto the beach, he ducked into the shadow of its seaward side, crept forward until he was level with the mule team and slipped under the traces. By then they were in the middle of a heaving, shouting throng of horses, carts and drivers. Carswell forced himself between the two rear mules, their flanks lathered white with sweat, lowered his head, leaned against the yoke and pushed forward.

At the ramp, he heard further shouts and the crack of a whip. Water surged over his boots, the mules twisted and snorted, he caught a glimpse of a pair of uniformed legs, then, with a sudden clattering rush, the wagon skidded up the wooden platform and came to a stop in the hold. A few moments later there were more cries, a juddering thump from the stern and the ferry swung out into the stream.

A hundred yards from the shore, Carswell lifted his head and looked back. The two *guardias* were checking the groups of people who'd clustered round the jetty for the the ferry's return, while the other patrols were still pacing along the beach. He worked his way out between the mules' hindquarters, grinned at the wagon driver who'd come over to thank him, and settled against the forehatch to wait for the landing.

He found the gypsy as soon as they'd unloaded the wagon on the other side, Carswell thanked him again and helped Minette up onto the mule.

As he settled her across the animal's back with her legs hanging down in front of the panniers, there was a sudden shout from behind them. Minette turned to look over her shoulder.

'What's that?'

Carswell raised his head. The space between the water and the trees was a single waist-high cloud of dust. Through it he could see the trotting horses of the Sanlúcar brotherhood. Behind them the carts and wagons and caravans were beginning to roll forward, and further back still the pilgrims on foot were joining the procession.

'*Viva la Blanca Paloma—!*'

The shout came again—the call to the "white dove" of the marshes. Then, from a thousand voices behind the fluttering banner of the outrider at the squadron's head, the answering shout.

'*Viva!*'

'*Viva la Virgen del Rocio!*'

'*Viva!*'

The sound was tumultuous now, echoing along the shore as the head of the procession wound into the trees.

'The start of the Rocio. You might as well get used to it, Minette—'

Carswell bent back over the mule's girth.

'You're going to hear it solid for five days and nights—and a hell of a lot besides!'

18

Coto Doñana

Sand first. Then the trees with the long flat corridors of pale earth winding between them. Afterwards sand again—bare, white, heat-glazed now, rolling in great dunes to the horizon, where the sky, studded with wheeling kites and white as the sand, came down to meet it.

That was the first morning and afternoon as Carswell and the girl travelled steadily at the rear of the long chain of horsemen and carts uncoiling from the landing-points opposite Sanlúcar. One hundred thousand people moving through the *marismas* towards the little town on the northern border of the Coto. The constant, thickening, enveloping presence of the Rocio pilgrimage. And over them all the tunnel of dust, shot through with the steady beating of drums, the piping of flutes, the gleaming wine bottles thrown from hand to hand, the sudden galloping silhouettes of riders breaking from the column to chase some wild deer or boar through the trees before wheeling round, shouting and laughing, to take their places in the procession again.

At midday they stopped to eat. Afterwards there was nothing except the dunes, the occasional tiny blue flowers rooting in the whiteness, the windless heat and the column winding ahead. Carswell walked by the mule's bridle. It was too hot to talk, although he'd turn from time to time and glance back to Minette. She'd nod and smile and he'd go on.

Somewhere in front of them Samir would be lying asleep on the second floor of the *palacio,* the morning's hunting over and the hot hours of the afternoon come. Carswell remembered the white stallion, its movements, its conformation, the falcon on the man's wrist. He thought of the light on the silver hawk bells and the sound of the bells chiming and the man's laughter. Then he shook his head, clearing the images from his mind.

As the light waned, they came to the plain of scrub he remembered vividly from his visit to the Coto five days before. The dunes ended and the track became a single lane through the rosemary bushes, the smell of the crushed herb overwhelming now after the passage of the carts and horsemen, and the powdered branches gleaming with the papery yellow flowers of marsh cistus. Afterwards, there was darkness, hazed with dust, the shapes of home-going birds, ice-white egrets and great wing-beating herons, lanterns on every side and the songs of the Rocio rippling back down the column.

Finally at ten they saw the lights of the *palacio*. Not the few bright windows he'd seen that night as he crawled through the bushes, but a ring of orange-red flares round them on the plain, the fires of the encampment. He turned off the track and stopped in a clearing where a dozen carts were drawn up round a fire.

Minette dismounted and rubbed her legs; her face was caked with sweat and dust.

'*Mon Dieu!*' She glanced towards the *palacio*. 'That where he is?'

Carswell nodded. He hobbled and fed the mule. Then he unloaded the panniers, opened them and took out the three hawks.

All three were still encased in the lengths of stocking with only their feet protruding at one end. He cut some branches from a bush, stripped them of their leaves, bound them into a rough frame and drove the sharpened ends into the earth. The two cross-bars were a few inches from the ground, forming a crude perch.

Then he filled a shallow metal bowl with water, built up a

platform of stones by the frame and rested the bowl on top so that its rim was eight inches above the cross-bar. He picked up the first bird, the big female peregrine, settled its feet on the perch and waited until its claws had tightened round the bar. Then he rolled down the end of the stocking so that its head was exposed.

For a few moments it rocked there precariously, its yellow eyes blinking into the surrounding darkness. Then it managed to balance itself and settled down, beak just above the bowl of water. Carswell walked back a short distance, squatted on his heels and watched. It was ten minutes before the bird lowered its head, and took a cautious sip. Afterwards it began to gulp thirstily.

When it had finished, Carswell cut a small piece of meat from a roll of *chorizo* and dropped it into the tray. This time the hawk didn't hesitate; this was the first food in two days, and it snapped forward, almost toppling off the perch. There was a sharp tap as its beak struck the metal, a tearing sound and then the bird was upright once more, twisting its head round as it swallowed. The scrap wasn't anything like enough to satisfy its hunger, but combined with the water it would serve Carswell's purpose—to keep the bird alive and ravenous until he was ready.

Half an hour later he'd gone through the same routine with the merlin and the male peregrine. The peregrine responded just as the first one had done; the merlin drank the water but refused the meat. Its eyes were slightly dull and the skin on its legs was slack when Carswell touched them. The bird might have been coming into moult, but more likely the traumatic experience of its capture, coupled with the heat and the confinement in the stocking, had proved too much; he wondered whether it would last through the next day.

Carswell put all three carefully back in the pannier, left the lid half open for air and stood up. Minette, who'd been unpacking when he'd started, had disappeared. As he peered into darkness, the sound of a guitar came from the direction of a fire, followed by the chorus of a song. It ended and he heard a peal of laughter.

He walked over to the fire and found her sitting with a group of gypsies. Her arms were round two of the men and the guitarist was trying to teach her the words of the song.

'Hey, Carswell, listen—'

She jogged the guitarist, beckoned him to play and sang the opening phrase of a paso doble, breaking off to a round of cheering.

'Isn't that something?' Minette patted the ground. 'Come on, sit down. I'll teach you too.'

It was two o'clock before they went back to the panniers.

Carswell spread out a blanket and they lay with their arms round each other for warmth, the bushes knotty and resinous against their backs and the lights of the fires gleaming across the clearing. Occasionally a late-coming horseman passed along the track, and throughout the night distant flutes and drums beat out the long passages of flamenco.

Carswell woke at four, feeling the rising damp as mist coiled over them. The fire had died down; on every side tethered animals snorted and tugged at their halters. Somewhere a wild cat screamed. He turned to settle himself more comfortably and noticed Minette's eyes were open.

'Cold?'

Her head touched his shoulder as she nodded.

'Come closer.'

Carswell pulled her towards him and held her tightly.

'Christ, wasn't that good tonight?' she said.

'Didn't I tell you Rocio was a party?'

'It's something—I don't know—just something you can't really say, isn't it? Except—'

The words were so quiet he could barely hear her.

'*Merde*. If we could just go on with them tomorrow. If it was different, a real holiday, the way it is for them.'

'We will go on tomorrow. Even if this man's here, I can't finish what Jean was doing until we're on the way back.'

'It's not that. Hell, you know what I mean, just if it was different.'

'Maybe next year it will be. Maybe we can do it properly. A horse for me, that damn dress for you, even a cart—'

'Next year? Who are you kidding, Carswell? Sure, I'd like to do it again. But there'll be someone else. Hell, there are loads of girls you could pick up and screw and take with you. Me too; I'll probably have another fellow then.'

He smiled. 'Knowing you, Minette, I certainly wouldn't bet against it.'

'So why next year? What's wrong with this one?'

'Nothing—'

Carswell stopped. There was nothing wrong with this year. Over the past ten days it had opened, changed, split apart like a nut cracked by a hammer—Minette's chestnut tapped at the crown with the shell splintering to expose the kernel inside.

He didn't yet know fully what that kernel was, except that it represented something fundamentally different from all the cold dry years of the past. And it included Minette. Not for ever; permanence, constancy, stability ran directly counter to everything she was. Carswell knew that, knew one morning he'd wake and she'd be gone with the same unannounced suddenness she'd entered his life.

It didn't matter; whether it happened in a week or a year, nothing could ever be the same again. No, there was nothing wrong with this year—once the serial had been completed.

Minette shook her head and broke the silence. 'You still want to go on with it, don't you? You're wrong, Carswell. You can't have it both ways. It won't work, I promise you. At least Jean was the same come anything. You're not; there's that bit in the centre, and it'll all go to bits and—'

She paused. Then she laughed as if she were dismissing everything she'd said, and snuggled closer to him.

'Never mind. We've got three days. Let's make them as good as tonight.'

She was asleep again almost immediately. Soon afterwards Carswell slept too.

The Land-Rovers drove into the forecourt of the *palacio* at six. Carswell woke instantly, slid out from under the blanket without waking Minette, crossed the clearing and worked his way through the bushes until he reached the edge of the open stretch of plain.

He was much closer to the building than before and the mist was lighter. As he watched, the horsemen came out through the arch above the main gates; the two mounted Arabs, the Coto ranger, the thick-set American, and this time a groom with the white stallion, riderless, behind him. They trotted past him and vanished into the mist, heading towards the dunes.

A few minutes later the first of the Land-Rovers appeared. There'd been three before; now there were five. It was still too dim for Carswell to see him, but he knew that one of the extra vehicles contained Samir. The fifth probably carried an additional complement of guards. They drove across the turf, leaving dark tracks in the dew-laden grass, and vanished in the same direction as the riders.

Carswell waited until the sound of the engines faded. Then he walked back to the clearing. Wisps of smoke were rising all round him from the dead fires of the night's encampment. The dawn air smelt crisp and clean, and people were beginning to saddle up for the day's ride to Rocio. Minette stirred, yawned and lifted herself sleepily on one elbow as he reached the panniers.

'Were you right, Carswell?'

He nodded, knelt down and closed the lid of the pannier which held the hawks.

'They're not letting him ride until he's well away from all

this,' he said. 'But once they get to the dunes, it'll be just like it was when I watched him before. A few more guards, that's the only difference. Otherwise, it's the same.'

She shook her head slowly. 'I wish to Christ it wasn't.'

'Well, you can forget about it until Tuesday.' He smiled at her over the wickerwork. 'We've got Rocio first.'

The three days, and the two nights between them, ran into a single continuum of movement, dust, horses, music, wine and laughter.

They reached Rocio that evening, travelling all day behind the southern brotherhoods as they'd done the day before. There was another stretch of isolated trees, their branches cracking under the weight of the mud nests of colonies of storks, bushes teeming with golden orioles, deer running rose-coloured and chequered with shadow, a heat haze over the mud flats of the estuary to their right, then, in the late afternoon, the coolness of a eucalyptus forest.

Finally, at dusk, the town itself. From every direction now other columns of horsemen, carts, wagons, caravans, pilgrims on foot; packing the trails to the north and west and east, pouring in across the low marshy fields, lining the horizon in an unending skein of noise and colour.

For Carswell it meant safety. The ghost town of Rocio was alive with the presence of a hundred thousand people, an immense raucous concourse in which they were hidden, anonymous, part of the great single brotherhood of the pilgrimage. No one would look for or find them there.

To Minette it was something different. He was unable to forget for an instant that at the end of it all was Samir, the dunes, the imprisoned hawks, the gun-shot. She seemed to ignore that entirely, treating the time as a holiday, drinking, talking, laughing as he'd never seen her before.

They slept in the gypsy encampment outside the walls. There

were rockets throughout the night, sudden cracks of sound behind the golden flares. Rockets and flutes and the interminable beating of the drums. Even in the grey light of dawn, when Carswell woke, the rockets were still exploding and the drums throbbing.

They walked all Sunday through the streets of the town, swirling with chalk-white dust and filled with the thunder of hoofs. They watched the last of the brotherhoods arrive, the black mountain horses from the sierra villages and the towering ox-carts from Sevilla. They went to the church, Minette crossing herself and waiting behind the kneeling penitents who left snail-tracks on the sandy floor as they crawled to the altar, and stood gazing at the Virgin—heavy, wooden, looking out with implacable black eyes.

At midnight they bought candles and joined the torchlight procession that would file in vigil round the town all night, pacing slowly in the darkness, with the lanterns veining every street. Afterwards, they visited the fair-ground off the main square. Carswell lost Minette for a time. When she reappeared she was wearing an embroidered shawl and her hair had been braided.

She swung round in front of him laughing.

'Look, Carswell!'

'Where the hell did you get that?'

She gestured behind her. 'A family over there. I went and talked to them, and the lady did my hair and then she made me take this. I told her I never got time to buy a dress, so she said it was a present.'

'What do you mean you talked to them? You can't speak—'

'In Rocio I can!'

Minette seized his hand, dragged him into one of the flamenco bars and made him sit watching her while she danced.

The next day was Monday. Carswell woke early. He sat up and listened. It was still dark but he could hear the noises of the encampment being broken up. Horses were being saddled, mules harnessed to carts, crates packed and roped down, fires fanned to life for the last time.

The Virgin still had to be paraded round the town. That would happen during the morning and by midday she would be back on her throne in the church. The Rocio was almost over and the cavalcade was preparing to disperse.

Before nightfall they'd be outside the *palacio* once more, on the final stage of the journey.

'I'm going to need you with me, Minette—'

Carswell was squatting by a fire he'd lit a few minutes earlier. Two hundred yards behind him the lights of the *palacio* were shining through the darkness and on every side there was the glow of other fires, lit by the returning horsemen as they settled down for the last night of the pilgrimage.

'Not for long. Just to look after the mule while I get it set up so I'm sure.'

'Sure of what?'

The outline had been clear in Carswell's mind since he'd seen the Rocio emblem in the newspaper, but one critical element had been missing. He hadn't even realized what it was until they passed an open cart on the outskirts of Rocio, where a gypsy was selling provisions to the home-going riders. Something had fluttered in a cage hanging from the cart's axle. They were fifty yards further on before he realized what it was. Then he'd turned and gone back.

'Sure that he gets the chance to do what I want,' Carswell said. 'That's what I'd left out before and that's why I bought those—'

He pointed at a wood-slatted cage on the ground beside the panniers.

Inside, huddled on the floor, were the four wild partridges he'd bought from the gypsy. He'd counted on Samir putting up a bird of his own accord, just as he'd done the day Carswell watched him from the thicket. It would almost certainly still happen: the dunes were thick with game, there must have been two dozen carcasses dangling from the back of the Land-Rover on its return to the *palacio* after the day's hunting and it was inconceivable the morning would pass without Samir being able to loose the falcon.

The likelihood wasn't enough. Carswell needed to be certain —and certain not just that it would happen, but happen at the place he chose. That was even more important now in view of the extra guards. The partridges provided the answer.

Minette glanced at the cage. Then she looked back at the fire. She said nothing.

'Look, if I thought there'd be any danger for you—'

'Danger?' Her head jerked up. 'You think that's what's screwing me up? I don't care a fuck about danger!'

'What is it then?'

'You, that's what. You and what you're doing and what you shouldn't be doing—'

She leant forward and gripped his wrist.

There was silence for several moments. In the firelight he could see the roots of her hair were turning black as the bleach grew out. Her skin was brown and her eyes were dark, unblinking, intense.

He shook his head. 'I'm sorry, Minette.'

'Oh, Christ—!'

She dropped his wrist wearily and turned away.

'What do you want me to do with that mule?'

He explained, she nodded, then she lay down by the fire. It was ten o'clock. According to Carswell's calculations they wouldn't need to leave until midnight.

Carswell sat smoking for a time. Then he tossed his cigarette into the bushes and lay down beside her. She stiffened and rolled away. A few moments later she suddenly turned and moved back.

'Sorry, Carswell. Here—'

She put her arms round him and rested her face against his. 'Whatever I think, I'd still buy you as a hot-water bottle!' He laughed and they both dozed until it was time to leave.

Carswell settled the panniers over the mule, helped Minette onto the animal's back, with the cage of partridges resting on the pommel in front of her, and they set off.

It was an hour's walk to the edge of the dunes. The night was clear and starry. Gradually the sound and fires of the encampment faded behind them and there was nothing except the scent of rosemary lifting from the ground, the crescent of a new moon rising overhead and the creak of the mule's harness. As they reached the end of the plain, a fifteen-foot wall of sand reared above them. Carswell handed Minette the halter and walked forward to the dune's crest.

Behind him the plain stretched for over three miles to the *palacio,* a broad corridor of grass and shrub studded by the occasional thicket and walled on either side by trees. Ahead the sand rolled away as far as he could see under the night sky; there were further dunes, curling like frozen waves in the darkness, low hillocks, long level stretches between the ridges, and everywhere stunted clumps of reed and desert grass.

For a mounted falconer it was the ideal hunting landscape; a firm surface underfoot for a galloping horse, limitless cover for game-birds in the little scattered bushes and the whole set in a strictly guarded preserve that stretched twenty miles from where he was standing. Looking over it now for the first time, Carswell realized that LeKahn's guess wasn't only right; once he'd had the trigger of the hawk's shadow, it was inevitable.

Carswell turned and walked back to the mule.

'It'll take us about twenty minutes to get there,' he said. 'Then I'll need an hour to set the thing up. Afterwards, it's just a question of waiting.'

He took the halter, turned the mule's head so they were parallel to the dunes and pulled the animal behind him towards the trees.

They were a quarter of a mile into the wood when he stopped again. The plain was behind them now, the dunes immediately to their right and somewhere in the distance to the south the Sanlúcar landing-point. Carswell took out his knife, found a cluster of saplings and cut off an armful of long supple branches.

Then he rummaged in the pannier for a ball of cord and dropped it into his pocket.

'You'll be more comfortable if you get off—'

She shrugged as he lifted down the cage of partridges, swung her leg over the mule's back and dropped to the ground.

'Can I have a cigarette?'

He gave her the last pack in the carton. 'You know what to do if one of the rangers appears?'

She nodded. 'Just say "Rociero" and then—what's "husband" again?'

'*Marido.*'

'*Marido.*' She repeated the word twice. 'I say that and point as if I'm waiting for you to come back.'

'That's it. I don't think it's likely or we'd have seen one by now; they're probably on the other side watching the river. Anyway—'

Carswell arranged the bundle of saplings under his arm and picked up the wooden cage.

'I'll be as quick as I can.'

It took him longer than he'd thought to find the right clump of reed and thorn, a spiney circle of brush under the lee of a small hillock thirty yards into the dunes. He put down the cage, pulled out his knife and the ball of cord, and set to work.

It took him an hour. First he carved a space out of the centre of the thorn. Then he constructed a bee-hive-shaped basket with the saplings—strong enough to hold the partridges if they fluttered against it, but with a bent-wood latch at the top which would slip and allow the whole structure to spring to pieces when the cord was pulled.

Three times he tried the latch before he was satisfied. Afterwards he clipped it back into place, transferred the birds from the cage to the sandy floor at the basket's base, tucked the last sapling under the latch and knotted the cord over it. Finally, he began to pay out the line, walking backwards away from the clump of thorn and stopping every yard to cover the cord with sand.

By the time he reached the trees he was sweating.

Minette was sitting down waiting for his return. He saw the glow of her cigarette close to the ground as he worked his way carefully between the trunks, then the outline of her head against the sky as she stood up. He tied the end of the cord round a bush and wiped his face. He could hear the sound of the mule's jaws cropping grass.

'All right,' he said. 'That's it. What time have you got?'

'Ten past three.'

There was a tiny green glow as she lifted her wrist. Carswell looked at his own watch.

'Right. And you're quite clear on what you do?'

'Yes.'

'Let's go through it once more—'

Her instructions were simple enough and he'd made her repeat them several times before they left the encampment by the *palacio*.

The track which led from the *palacio* to the Sanlúcar landing-point was an hour behind them through the wood. Carswell would set her on the mule with the last of their provisions, turn her to face the east and give the animal its head. There was no need for Minette to worry about finding her way between the trees; the mule would do that for her. As soon as she reached the track she was to dismount, tether the animal and sleep until daylight.

When dawn came it would simply be a matter of following the tail-end of the returning procession until she arrived at the jetty opposite Sanlúcar. She'd reach it in the mid-afternoon and she was to wait there until the last ferry docked at dusk. If

Carswell hadn't joined her ten minutes before it left on the homeward journey, it would mean something had gone wrong and she was on her own.

He'd given her his passport with her name inside as his wife, all of his remaining money and instructions on what to do on the other side. A bus to Algeciras, the ferry across to Tangier, a flight from there to Paris—the same sequence he'd told her to follow in the Sevilla hotel. The chance of her getting away then had been remote. Now it was much stronger. Until he'd been fired on by the *guardias,* Carswell had assumed she'd be the main target of the police hunt. The shots in the Barrio de Santa Cruz had proved him wrong.

Somehow, and still inexplicably, he seemed to be the one they were after, not her. Now, with passport and money, she might make it by herself.

'No more questions—?'

Minette shook her head.

'All right, let's have your leg—'

Carswell heaved her onto the mule's back, removed the guncase from one pannier and the two peregrines from the other; the merlin had died that morning and he'd dropped its body, still encased in the woolen sock, in a ditch outside Rocio.

'Take care, Carswell.'

She was looking down at him, her head silhouetted against the sky in a gap between the branches.

'You too.'

'I will—and don't—'

'Don't take any chances?' Carswell shook his head, smiling. He tapped the gun-case.

'Promise?'

'Promise!'

He balanced the two hawks in the cradle of his arm and came round to the saddle to kiss her.

'No.' Minette leant back. 'Things like that, they're for goodbye. Kiss me when you see me again at the ferry. Christ—!'

The mule had been tossing its head, jangling the bridle and pulling at the reins. Now it made a sudden obdurate movement into the trees.

'This fucking animal!'

Carswell slapped its haunch and watched them disappear into the darkness. He stood for a few moments listening to her voice cursing. Then he walked away.

An hour later he'd crossed the plain, entered the woodland on the far side and settled himself down in the bushes at its edge. By then Minette was two or three miles to the south, still surrounded by trees and separated from him by the open funnel of turf and scrub that ran back to the *palacio* between the two areas of forest. In front of Carswell was a bare space of sand with the dunes rising beyond.

Sometime shortly before midday Samir would appear on the crest of the first dune and ride down towards him. For the following ten minutes the Arab would be alone between the sand and the trees.

Guesswork. It was all guesswork. Yet it had been like that from the start of his involvement in the Robespierre serial. The guess that LeKahn had discovered Samir's hiding-place; the guess that Minette knew it too; the guess that the Arab wouldn't tolerate being moved during the Rocio pilgrimage; so many more. Each one had proved right. Now there was the final guess—that at midday Samir would come over the crest alone.

The reason involved a simple equation between the nature of falconry and the time of the year. The long-winged raptors, the classic hunting birds that Samir was working, would only fly at game with a rising or a westering sun behind them. When the sun reached its zenith, and throughout the hot afternoon hours, they'd refuse to stoop. In late May the sun over the *marismas* climbed to its highest pitch just after noon.

The hunting party would drive the dunes all morning, tracing a half-circle so that they kept the rising sun behind them. By eleven, with only an hour of the morning's chase left, they'd have reached the southern tip of the Coto. They'd turn and start a final sweep up the edge of the dunes which would bring them to the mouth of the plain just before midday—when they'd swing right and ride back across the turf to the *palacio*.

That had been the pattern when Carswell had watched them from the thicket. It had taken him some time to work out its significance. As soon as he'd done so, he knew it would be the same every day. What happened when the foreleg of the flanking horseman struck the cord and released the partridges was something quite different—and unpredictable.

When the basket of saplings disintegrated and the birds fluttered up from the circle of thorn, the riders would be trotting in line, with the Land-Rovers fifty yards behind. The partridges' first reaction would be to fly north—away from the sun and towards Carswell. Providing Samir's falcon wasn't already at flight, the Arab would loose it immediately.

The partridges would then either go to ground in another clump of thorn, in which case the horsemen would put them up again, or keep desperately heading north. Either way, as soon as they were level with the wood, they'd veer abruptly to the right, skim down over the dune and try to take cover in the trees round Carswell. Samir's falcon would stoop somewhere between the first circle of thorn and the trees; the distance from the sapling basket to where Carswell was lying was no more than a mile; if he'd calculated correctly, the hawk would strike in the final open stretch of sand before the wood.

From the start the crucial problem had been to separate Samir from both the other horsemen and the Land-Rovers when his falcon stooped. That was why Carswell had taken the two wild peregrines from Castellar. It was impossible to be certain what would happen when he rolled off the woolen stockings and tossed the ravenous birds into the air. But if they behaved as he guessed—soaring first up the warm air currents of the dunes, sighting the partridges and striking at them too—then he knew how Samir would react.

The little Arab had done it a week earlier when the marsh harrier had attacked the bird he'd just put up for his own falcon. He'd wave the others back, forbidding them to move from where they were, and ride forward alone. Ride to the crest of the dune and then down the slope on the far side towards the bushes where Carswell would be lying in the shadow with the Mannlicher in front of him.

Ten minutes. That was all Carswell needed. The single shot, then those ten minutes to put a mile between himself and the edge of the woods before the first of the following horsemen galloped forward to see what had happened. A quarter of an hour later he'd be back on the track to the Sanlúcar landing-point—anonymous in the stream of the returning Rocio pilgrims.

Carswell glanced at his watch: five o'clock, an hour and a half before he'd hear the Land-Rovers. The gun-case was on one side of him in the undergrowth, the two peregrines, rustling occasionally against their tight woolen bonds, on the other.

He lay back, crossed his arms behind his head and watched the stars between the leaves. Later he slept.

The convoy went by just after six-thirty.

Carswell woke to the sound of engines and the rattle of bridles a few hundred yards away through the trees. The light was grey with dawn and there was thick mist again. He listened as the noise changed from the crunching of wheels and hoofs through the scrub to a softer slurred sound as the procession reached the sand. One of the Land-Rovers seemed to break away from the party and drive north along the gulley beyond the dune to his right. Otherwise the pattern was as before.

He waited until all the sounds had vanished. Then he opened the gun-case, assembled the Mannlicher and crawled forward until he was at the extreme edge of the wood, with the bare sand shelving up in front of him to the dune's crest. He found a thick hawthorn bush, collected the peregrines and worked his way in among the tangled roots.

Once he'd cleared some of the branches with his knife, it was like lying inside a small cave. He eased the rifle forward, clipped on the telescopic sight and raised the stripped butt to his shoulder. By then the sun had risen and the mist was clearing quickly. Even without the magnification of the reflex lens he could see every yard of sand between the bush and the ridge. Through the sight he could pick out the dew on the petals of a cluster of tiny pale-blue flowers just below the crest and then, as he focused more sharply still, the movement of a column of ants behind.

Carswell swung the Mannlicher slowly from side to side, trimmed some more branches, checked again and lowered the gun to the ground. He had an uninterrupted view not just of the section of dune immediately ahead, but for two hundred yards in either direction. He nudged up the quivering bundles of the imprisoned falcons until they were lying beside the barrel. Then he rested his chin on his hands and waited.

A little under five hours and it would be over. The mission he still knew only by its stencilled code-name, the Robespierre serial, which for three weeks had been his entire world, reduced finally to the moment when the little Arab appeared on the crest and rode down towards him—the moment when he lifted the Mannlicher again, aligned the needle-thin reference bars in the sight, exhaled and squeezed the trigger.

Everything in the end coming down to that. The week he'd followed LeKahn from Marseilles to the Guadalajara mountains; the walk through the hills with Minette trudging sullen and bloody-footed behind him; the days in the little hotel, clean and white and sun-filled, as their strength came back; his reconnaissance of the Coto, the wild hawks of Castellar, the drums and rockets, the dust and wine and galloping horses of Rocio; now at the last a hawthorn bush on the rim of the dunes.

It didn't even matter if he'd miscalculated, if the complex chain of triggers failed to work, if Samir didn't come. Whatever happened, he'd kept faith. Minette had been wrong. Minette—even thinking of her made Carswell smile. He shook his head and grinned. Afterwards the morning passed quickly.

The sun rose and the heat grew more intense with every hour. Occasionally he heard distant shouts, carried faintly on the light wind from the direction of the *palacio*—a returning Rociero calling drunkenly to his companions. A fallow deer, disturbed by some far-off horseman, cantered silently through the trees and vanished over the ridge, its feet leaving a lacework of delicate prints in the sand. A flock of egrets planed down, into the branches above his head, perched for a moment, then rose again—nine white arrows against the sky.

Sweat gathered on his forehead, pooling there so that he had to keep brushing it away before it trickled into his eyes, and the dune dazzled in the light.

'*Astaad! Astaad—!*'

The cry was thin but clear. Carswell recognized it from before—the Arab warning call that a game-bird had taken to the air.

He glanced down at his watch. It was a purely instinctive response because he'd been looking at the dial every few minutes for the past half hour: five to twelve. He knew the time anyway from the sun's angle. But he'd been right—the riders had swept the perimeter of the sand, one of the horses had tripped the cord and the partridges had been released.

He picked up one of the peregrines, gripped it by the feet and stripped off the woolen stocking. For an instant its wings beat furiously against his wrist and he could feel the surging pent-up energy in its body as the binding came loose and it fought to free itself from his hand. Then he opened his fingers, there was a blaze of brown-and-white-barred feathers and a dark sickle-shaped shadow on the sand—smaller every second as the bird soared upwards.

Carswell waited a further minute. Then he released the second hawk. His palm was bright with blood from a cut slashed by the talons of the first peregrine as it flew free, both shadows had vanished from the shimmering surface of the dune and his face was running with sweat.

He lowered his head, wiped his eyes against his sleeve and picked up the Mannlicher, holding it cradled in his arms with the butt under his shoulder. From now on he was working blind, with no possibility of knowing what was happening over the crest and out of his sight to the left.

If he was still right, if the whole elaborate structure of sunlight, falcon, timing and pride fused at the moment he'd planned for, then within the next few minutes a mounted silhouette, face hooded by the Arab head-dress, would appear somewhere above him on the ridge.

Carswell was right. The shadow came first—tiny, black on the whiteness of the sand, cast by the falcon towering high at pitch in the pale midday sky. Then the partridges, all four of them, skimming the dune, beating frenziedly downwards before they plunged into a clump of reeds midway between the crest and the wood. Finally, there was Samir.

Carswell lifted the gun and centred him in the sight. The Arab had appeared further to the left than he'd guessed. He trotted along the crest, paused uncertainly for a moment, then saw the reeds and came forward again. His golden head-band was glittering in the sun and the stallion's mane belled out, grey-white and shining in the light.

As Samir neared the reeds he reined in the horse and looked up—searching the sky for the falcon somewhere above him. Carswell could see him clearly now, eyes narrowed at the sun, face clear of the hood's shadow. He was calling—calling to the hawk—and he was laughing.

The hawk's shadow grew larger as the bird planed down. Samir kicked at the stallion's flanks and cantered suddenly into the reeds. The partridges rose again, swerved and jinked desperately, the falcon stooped, a lashing talon grazed a dun-coloured back and a barred feather spun in the air. Then the hawk's shadow was shrinking again as it climbed and the partridges were clattering into the safety of the branches of the trees.

Samir waited a moment. Then he wheeled the stallion and galloped back up the slope. He was still laughing.

Carswell lowered the gun. For almost two minutes he'd held the Arab at point-blank range in the hairline cross of the sight. He hadn't fired and he didn't fire now as Samir's back disappeared over the dune's crest.

It was the laughter. The laughter which linked him to Minette and at that final moment them both to the Arab. To have fired then, to have shattered that jewelled laughing figure would have been to return to the numb barren world in which Carswell had lived for so long. It would have meant denying the past three weeks, dismissing Minette's existence and disowning himself.

He couldn't do it. It was time now not to go back—but to go on. For a moment Carswell shook his head dizzily. Then he dismantled the Mannlicher, hid it in the roots of the bush, slid back onto the turf and arranged the branches to hide the tunnel entrance.

Finally he turned and began to walk back through the wood to the track that led to the Sanlúcar landing-point.

19

Sanlúcar

It took Carswell an hour to reach the end of the wood. Once he heard the sound of engines and the drumming of horses' hoofs through the trees to his right; it was the procession crossing the plain on its way back to the *palacio*. He waited in a glade until the noise had died away. Then he went on.

Finally he saw the track in front of him. He knelt down, crawled forward through the undergrowth and looked out. The *palacio* was a hundred yards ahead, white and still and silent under the blazing sun. The Land-Rovers and horses had been taken into the rear courtyard, the windows were shuttered against the heat and there was no sign of life anywhere. In one of the upstairs rooms, as Carswell had imagined him on the way out, Samir was probably already asleep.

Yet his guards, the burly shirt-sleeved men with shoulder holsters bulging under their arms, would still be watching hidden in the out-buildings. There was no reason for them to take any interest in Carswell—he'd be just another pilgrim returning on foot across the marshes—but there was no point in taking even the smallest chance now. He waited until a lumbering supply cart appeared from the direction of Rocio, let it draw abreast of the bushes where he was lying, then he stood up and ambled alongside it across the plain—invisible from the *palacio* behind the high canvas hood.

Twenty minutes afterwards he was in the trees on the far side and the building had disappeared.

It was after seven before the landing-point came into sight. By then the air was greying slightly and across the estuary the roofs of Sanlúcar were glowing in the evening light. Carswell followed the pine-covered ridge above the sweep of sand that ran down to the water until he was level with the ferry. Although it was only an hour before the last boat left, the pier was still thronged with horses, pilgrims and carts. He stopped and began searching through the crowd for Minette.

She must have been watching the ridge for him to appear, because she spotted him first. An arm waved at the edge of the crowd and she appeared on the sand. For a moment Carswell gazed at her as she came forward, tall, sun-tanned, laughing as she swore at the recalcitrant mule stumbling behind her. An overpowering sense of delight and exhilaration swept over him. He had been right: everything had changed and this was only the start.

Then he set off down the slope towards her.

'Carswell! You made it and it's over and it's fine, right?'

Carswell nodded smiling. 'It's fine, Minette.'

'Christ—!'

The mule stopped suddenly, dug its feet in and brayed, almost pulling the halter out of her hand.

'What do you think I am? A bloody groom or something? Here—'

She was a few yards away, still laughing as she threw him the rope.

'You see, I told you, didn't I? Oh Christ, Carswell, I'm glad, I'm happy—'

They were standing together now, the mule's head between them. Carswell picked up the halter, tugged the animal aside, bent forward to kiss her—and suddenly whirled away.

It was a reflex response, the product of those same thirty years of constant knife-edge alertness that had made him instinctively chop down the posada manager three weeks before.

This time it was something at the extreme limit of his vision, something that gleamed momentarily, metallic and oily, up in the pine trees he'd just left.

The first shot came before he'd even located it. A tiny spark in the branches, a coil of smoke, a hollow crack that echoed along the shore. Instantly the mule shuddered and lurched against him, choking and bubbling blood through its nostrils as its head crashed into his stomach and knocked him to the ground.

The bullet, missing Carswell's chest by inches, had hit the animal in the brain. He tumbled over, spat sand from his mouth and scrambled to his feet.

'Minette, get down! For Christ's sake, get down—!'

She was standing on the other side of the mule's body, frozen, white-faced, bewildered. Carswell hurled himself at her arm. Then the sniper fired again.

The second bullet hissed over his head and hit Minette at the base of her neck. She jerked back as if she'd been clubbed and toppled over. Carswell caught her as she fell, dragged her into the shelter of the mule's body and lay there with her head cradled in his lap.

Afterwards there were moments of total confusion. Screams from the ferry-point, horses rearing and plunging, cart-wheels grating as they churned in the water, people throwing themselves on the sand or racing desperately for the protection of the pier's wooden platform.

Carswell was only aware of it all as a dim background frenzy. He could smell the mule's sweat, feel the bristles of its hide pricking into his back, see its blood welling out over his knees. Minette was utterly still in his arms, eyes wide open—brown and puzzled and unblinking—her shirt, the shirt he'd bought her in Sevilla, stained dark from the jagged wound below her chin, lips moving slowly.

He lowered his head, trying to hear what she was saying,

holding her tight against him, stroking her hair in a meaningless comforting gesture. There was nothing except the silent painful working of her mouth.

'It'll be all right, Minette, I promise you—'

He spoke gently and quietly but with an urgent driving intensity, as if the words could somehow dissolve the nightmare that had suddenly enveloped them.

'Don't worry, it's going to be all right—'

She watched him for an instant, eyes still steady and bewildered. Then she seemed to shake her head slightly, shivered like the mule had done and went limp.

'Carswell! Carswell—!'

Carswell hadn't noticed the man. He must have run forward from the crowd by the landing-point. Now he stood above them, young, tallow-haired, face twitching, incongruous in his neat dark suit against the swirling dust and the still-rearing silhouettes of the horses at the water's edge beyond.

'You are Carswell, aren't you—?'

Carswell looked up at him expressionlessly, saying nothing.

'My name's Spencer—'

Carswell recognized the voice then, the nervous hesitant voice at the other end of the line when he'd made his nightly reports at the start of the mission.

'You haven't been hurt, have you—?'

As Carswell shook his head, an expression of relief went over Spencer's face.

'Thank God for that! I was afraid there might have been the most horrible accident. There was an operational misunderstanding. We had to bring in supplementary security—'

He broke off and waved vaguely towards the trees where the Special Branch marksman had been posted.

'Everything's all right now,' he went on. 'We'll be able to sort it all out. Well, that's what London sent me down here to do. What about her, though—?'

Spencer pointed uncertainly at Minette.

On the shore the screams had stopped. People were lifting themselves from the sand, a group of *guardia civil* were running forward; on the ridge the sniper, flanked by two of the Coto rangers, was silhouetted against the darkening sky.

Carswell slowly looked round. Then he lifted Minette's head from his lap, settled it carefully in the space hollowed out by his heels and stood up.

'Look, Carswell, don't worry about her—'

Spencer was watching him, frowning, his eyes narrowed and the nervous tick still plucking at the corner of his mouth.

'The Spanish police wanted her, anyway. You know, those two murders up in the north. We can deal with it all, really, I promise you. A bit of a muddle, but London's delighted with what you've done. Maybe it's even tidier like this—'

Carswell didn't hear him. He stepped forward, pushed Spencer aside and walked down the beach towards the water.

The light had gone now. Across the estuary the houses were shadowed as the sun dropped behind the rim of the marshes, and a new crescent moon lifted in the west. Carswell waded into the sea until the ripples were lapping round his waist.

Then he shut his eyes and stood there, smelling the salt and listening to the call of a late-hunting kestrel.